RILONDE

RILONDE

"This isn't just another rape story"

Murendeni Matumba

ISBN
978-0-620-95891-2(print)
978-0-620-95892-9(e-book)

I hope that one day you cannot help but stare in awe at me as you think to yourself "God surely does exist", I hope to be that beam of light for you, through the sharing of the art of my gift.

-Ms Rendy

Maybe this is based on a true story, or maybe this is based on the observations done on men and women, and the world in which they exist, or maybe, just maybe these are thoughts and opinions of a young woman who holds strong beliefs and has very big opinions about the world, but whatever it is, I hope you find it worth reading.

Contents

Introduction.. 1

Chapter 1: Introducing Rilonde 4

Chapter 2: The Men Are Trash Movement 13

Chapter 3: A Dose of Masculinity.............................. 24

Chapter 4: The Stereotype Is Real............................. 40

Chapter 5: My Parents Are Strict 52

Chapter 6: Welcome to The Rape Capital 63

Chapter 7: My History of Dating & Sexuality.............. 76

Chapter 8: The Encounter 105

Chapter 9: The Use of Words to Try and Explain 117

Chapter 10: Coming Out.. 131

Chapter 11: Triggered.. 151

Chapter 12: Changing the Narrative 175

Chapter 13: The Aftermath 207

Chapter 14: The Switch-Up..................................... 220

Chapter 15: Beholden to Grace............................... 236

Chapter 16: Does It Get Any Better? 250

Chapter 17: Messages to Her................................... 268

INTRODUCTION

The book "Rilonde" was inspired by a character that I created, who, like myself and many other South African women or women in the world around, has had an experience of some form of sexual assault, abuse & heartache, and seeks to share her story to not only console her fellow sisters and even brothers, but to also inspire healing and change.

The book is written in the first person POV (The main character, Rilonde, being the first person) although I, Murendeni Matumba, am the actual author of the book.

Since "Rilonde" translates to "Take care of", I saw it very fitting to use it as the title of the book, as it summarises all that is being expressed in this novel.

It isn't that people aren't open to being good and kind-hearted, it isn't that people cannot love and trust, it isn't that they cannot do good or be that, but having experienced so much harshness from the world, whether at a young age or at an older stage in life, it can become challenging and difficult to see oneself as worthy or deserving of love, respect or just affection from the human heart. I'll give you a more practical illustration; when a child experiences ill-treatment from their parents, friends, peers, or even strangers, they can feel "unloved", or just "worthless", or "undeserving of love and affection, not only from those respective individuals but from the world itself" and so, that child becomes closed off, closed off to the idea of anyone ever being able to love them the way they know their parents or peers should have, in fact, that child could take on and embody the insults that those individuals may have exchanged with them; "You are stupid or an idiot, you're ugly, you are a bastard child", and that can translate to them perhaps becoming a bully or just a really mean person, because how can a stupid person "think" to be nice to someone else? Or if I'm ugly, then that means that I am unlovable and if I'm unlovable, that means that I cannot give or receive love.

However, if someone notices that the same child has a beautiful voice and they tell that to them, or even better, they encourage them to sing and make them think of the possibility of them one day becoming a singer because that person recognises some potential in the child, that child becomes more confident because of the hope that individual has in them. They begin to sing a little louder than they normally would, and begin to have this boldness in them, to sing in a public space, and then it so happens that they are one day standing on top of a stage receiving an award for best artist, or being interviewed on their musical journey or career, or they share a post on some social media platform (because it doesn't have to be a really big platform like a big stage involving an award to give acknowledgement to someone), it could even be them just chatting to a friend or stranger, sharing a story of how a man or a woman believed so much in them when they didn't, and encouraged them to pursue this passion of singing, and they did, and that is how they got to where they are and that is all thanks to that person's faith in them and encouragement they gave to them. Same applies to people who are considered douchebags or scumbags, and people who are hurting from past pains or experiences, all of us were made to be good, made to experience goodness in every kind of way, but our environment can shape shift us into becoming miserable, terrible people, and of course, we cannot be saviours to other people but only to ourselves, but perhaps instead of calling these scumbags – "scumbags", or these hurt individuals – "victims" or "crazies", and just pointing out their faults and hurts, we can maybe open their hearts and eyes to the possibility of loving and being loved, the possibility of trusting and healing, through art or words of affirmation, and only hope that they can one day change and embody all those good stuff.

And I guess this is that book that offers endless possibilities to people, to help them realise how worthy of love and affection they are, how deserving they are of feeling a little lighter, and of feeling the joy and peace that comes with not hurting, as long as they are open to the idea and act of healing and can actively work towards that goal. This is that confirmation that they too can heal and can learn to fall in love with love again, with life too.

CHAPTER 1- INTRODUCING RILONDE

"Rilonde" is a Tshivenda word which translates to "Take Care Of".

Its original meaning is that of a prayer, a prayer to a God or a Heaven, to come down to earth, not literally, but to transcend an energy to the Earth and extend His hand to the pure in spirit, to keep them safe.

But in this book, the word speaks for itself; it is a call for security, safety, and reassurance.

A call to all of mankind to take on their responsibility to care for and protect our daughters & sons. It is a cry to Man to do away with the Rape/Abusive Culture.

-Ms Rendy

Allow me to introduce myself, will you?

My name is Rilonde, and this is my story...

Born in the Transvaal of Limpopo, I was named Rilonde by the woman who birthed my mother.

My mother had a home birth, and so my grandmother was present during my birth and assisted with my mother's birthing.

"Rilonde was exactly what her name suggested. When I first held her in my arms, I gazed into her tiny little eyes, she was filled with so much beauty on the inside-out; a beautiful little soul with eyes that glistened like the ocean, she was pure! Her kind and loving heart was visible through her joyous cry. I had to name her 'Rilonde' because a young one like her needed to be kept and taken good care of", proclaims my grandmother.

One can't say I grew up with any nasty childhood issues, but I was a bit challenged when it came to my self-esteem. Growing up and considered "a big girl" because I appeared to be a little older than most of my peers, due to my physicality and having gone through the changes of puberty that left my face acnefied, I felt a little different from the rest, as many would judge and tease me. I, however, remained confident of one thing, that the same Manufacturer who had carefully designed all my facial features, knitted every atom of my body, and permeated my soul with a breathful life, must look at me and see me as beautiful.

I grew up in a family of six, with two parents, two brothers, and one sister. I was most definitely a daddy's girl growing up, my mother worked as a nurse at the local clinic, whereas my father worked as an educator. I was the third out of my three siblings, born in a year considered the last year of the 90's kids. Both my mother and father ensured that we got the best out of life, we went to private schools from a very young age and got the best education, not to say that public schools do not offer great education, but just to put emphasis on the kind of education my siblings and I received from the schools that we went to.

Growing up, I could say that I was privileged, no, I did not grow up in a family that was financially loaded, but we had everything that we needed, from some over-the-top household necessities to the best education, we had it good. I was never a cool kid, or the kind of child who was reckless, and stout, and just in everyone's face, and that was because I grew up in a Christ centred family, a Christian family that is. Growing up, going to church meant we had Bible study on Saturdays, choir practice on Thursdays and Saturdays, and the actual church service on Sundays. I think growing up in the kind of family that I grew up in played a huge role in the kind of person that I am today, although most of my decisions are very much personal to me and not entirely influenced by my family values, my childhood background most definitely plays a huge role on those. Growing up, I had a lot of male friends, for some reason I clicked a lot with boys than I did with girls, I had a pretty cool relationship with all my friends, although at some point in high school most of them became my friends because they wanted more from me and I had to, unfortunately, put them in the "friendzone"- a term used to describe the act of befriending someone and not pursuing a romantic relationship with them, even though they may want more than just a friendship. But regardless of the friend zones; my friends and I maintained good friendships between us.

I was what you would consider a smart kid, I excelled well in school in terms of my studies, I played sports but more than anything, I enjoyed debate. I was a very shy, laid-back individual who didn't enjoy the attention of many pupils, but I always found so much confidence within myself when it came to debating, I enjoyed it, and I was great at it, I did well there too. My parents were determined to ensure that I enjoyed my school days, by ensuring that I partook in almost every activity that was available at school, and I enjoyed every minute of those experiences, and as a result of my engagement at school, there was no doubt that the educators at my school(both primary and high school), absolutely fell in love with me. I was loved, dearly by my educators, and they ensured that I was always on top of my game in every area of my school activities.

But even with such an amazing childhood, I had some traumas that I faced at a young age, in the four corners of my own home. In the safest space that a child or any individual considers safe and secure, I was molested. I first got molested at the age of 8, I did not understand what that was at the time, however, I did feel that it was wrong. It all started on a Friday evening when my mother and father had gone out to our grandparent's house for one of our uncle's funeral, Joseph. He was my father's brother. Malumi Joe had passed away in a car accident on his way back from work, he worked late-night shifts and would usually drive back home immediately after work even though he would be exhausted, and I guess on that faithful day he wasn't so lucky. I was left at home with my older brothers and little sister, both my brothers had their separate rooms, and my sister and I shared a room. My eldest brother was in his room talking on the phone with his then-girlfriend and as usual, the rest of us were watching soapies on the television just before bedtime, when my little sister who was five(5) at the time, decided that she was going to bed as she was exhausted, thus I was left with my older brother, Rothemba. After all the soapies were done airing, he decided that we should watch movies. Now, if you were the type to watch television late at night while growing up, you would know that the movies during that time needed to be censored as they included a lot of nudity. My brother at the time was around the age of 11, and that meant that we both had no business watching movies with an age restriction of 18, but there we were, watching. A few minutes in, of us watching the movie, which I cannot remember by name, my brother started to act "funny", or silly rather. He had his hand covering up the zipper of his pants, we were sitting on two different couches and so he came over to where I was seated, looked at me, and said, "we are going to play a game, a game where we do what 'Mommies and Daddies' do". I was so confused, but he asked me to nod to show that I understood and agreed, and I just nodded because I guess I was too young to understand, or perhaps I was coerced? Nevertheless, he began to touch my thighs, from my knees going all the way up to where my legs start or are conjoined to my upper body, he slid his hand "there", he touched me, I was nervous, but I didn't move, and the next thing he told me to do was to lie on my back, on the couch. I obliged, but before he could continue, our eldest brother came out of his room and it sounded as if he was approaching the lounge, so he told me to close my eyes and pretend as if I was fast asleep. I obliged to that too, he quickly changed the channel of the television, and when our older brother got to the lounge, Rothemba pretended to be carrying me to bed, as I was "sleeping". When we got to the bedroom, he whispered in my ear, don't tell anyone about our little game, it's between you and I, okay? I nodded and got inside my blankets, but I couldn't sleep that night. The following day we didn't talk about it, we both acted as if nothing had happened and went on with our lives.

However, that wasn't the only time. The next time it occurred was probably a few weeks following the incident. Because I was a daddy's girl, I enjoyed following my father around whenever he had his errands to run, and so did my brother. On one faithful day, my father had decided to go get quotes at the Hardware, for some wood he wanted to use for a project back at home, he left Themba and I in the car. It was a Sunday, and the town was not so busy with roaming people, when Themba tried to make a move on me, he touched me again, but fortunately enough he couldn't get that far with it because my father came rushing back into the car, as he had left his wallet, and wanted to ask that Themba and I come to help him carry some of the items he was going to purchase at the store.

Growing up, we used to play "House" a lot, and that was when Rothemba took advantage of the opportunity to "victimise" me. House was a game we used to play as kids, everyone around the block absolutely enjoyed it, we had our own little community of families, which consisted of mommies and daddies, children and sometimes grannies, aunts, uncles, and cousins, depending on the size of the group that was playing, it was so adorable, but the activities that went on in there? Shocking! It was quite interesting how such young kids would engage in these "sexual" activities, it came easy for them, as if it were normal, they enjoyed it, or perhaps I was the odd one out, but I never truly understood what the reason for that was, I never found pleasure in any of that, but because I had already had a taste of the poison, I was swayed into doing it.

Unfortunately, my experience with Themba was just the first of many to follow with men.

CHAPTER 2- THE "MEN ARE TRASH" MOVEMENT

DISCLAIMER: This is probably going to be "clickbait" for most, but before you decide on not continuing with your reading of this piece of information, I promise you that you will not regret reading this. This is just an opinion, some two cents from a female who is tired of hearing the same song on the radio over and over again, hoping to get a different tune or rather hoping they stop playing the song altogether, but nothing ever changes,

So here goes...

When a girl gets kidnapped, raped, bruised, murdered, or butchered, what is our first reaction? "Men are trash, men are dogs, men do not deserve to live", but have we ever sat down and thought of why men do the things they do? Well, one could argue that 'no, it's because men are raised by dogs, that is why they are dogs; how can a drunkard raise an any better human? How can a rapist raise someone who does not rape? Men do not have good role models to look up to!' But really, is it true now? Well, it could be, I mean don't get me wrong in any way, I am not trying to justify what most men have done to us women, to our daughters! But the truth of the matter is; no problem has ever been solved through the pointing of fingers.

We have so many platforms that expose women to the world, women are not afraid to be vulnerable and open about who they are and the experiences they encounter daily, be it emotionally or physically. But how many platforms do we have where men can openly talk about the stuff they go through mentally, or emotionally, even spiritually? Almost close to nil(or maybe I'm just unaware).

I want to say that "all men are trash", but we all know that that isn't entirely true (or well, I hope we all do). So, I'll take a step back and scrutinize some of the obvious reasons pointing to where this "men are trash" notion originates.

It must have originated from the time when one woman got sick and tired of the abusive & violent Masculine Being who bruised her fragile soul, or from the Female who was such a sucker for love and fell in love with what she thought was her soul mate but turned out to be the Beast who shattered her heart into unmendable pieces.

It could have come from the Feminal Being who got robbed of her dignity and safety by a thief who felt so entitled to what was not his, even after she had refused to give it to him, and she may have tried reporting him but his friends or family protected him, or they just went silent, neither denied nor accepted his actions, tried to shift the blame onto her and/or she was failed by the criminal justice system who concluded that her perpetrator was innocent as there wasn't enough evidence from her side to pin him down.

Maybe, just maybe, it came from the woman who was so loyal to a man who was still immature, still was looking to have fun, and could not settle for just one heart, and but although she would find out about his side hustles, she would stay, hoping that he would change but he never did, because he embraced disappointment so much that she could not take any more of it and decided to leave. But also,

It could've emerged from a time when a mother did not receive the full support she needed from her baby daddy, he may have refused paternal custody of his own baby, or he may have 'lost interest' in her and left her for a younger-looking female, because she never looked the same after her pregnancy, even though it is obvious to the eye that it is normal, that that is what happens to a woman's body after having carried another human being for months, it stretches, it definitely will not look like a silicone mannequin before, during, and after pregnancy and birth, it will have scars, increased fat, and a little weight gain and that is okay! Or maybe, just maybe it started with that very same baby who had a father who was never present in their life, so in order to fill the void created from the absence of fatherly love in her life, she tried to mingle with all different kinds of men to fill that void, only to end up creating a hole so deep that it left her feeling even more unworthy of a man's love, and left her feeling as if she did not need any man in her life, as "they are all just trash".

Perhaps it came from the mother who lost her daughter to some Masculine Being who decided to butcher her to death, and although she pleaded with him to stop, in pain, he ruthlessly sliced every part of her soul into pieces and left her lying there in cold blood, and although he may have admitted to doing it, and apologized for it, it could never change the fact that she is gone, never to return. Or,

It must have come from the female who was walking down the street, minding her own business, and came across a group of guys who began to speak to her i.e., catcalling; "hey beautiful, Nana, baby, my size, ausi wa mipako, Mabebeza", and she felt uncomfortable and irritated, so she chose to ignore them, because how dare they? But they just wouldn't leave it at that. Because she wouldn't entertain them, or let alone give them the attention they sought, they began to swear at her; "Ahh Fok, leave man, eintlik you're not even that beautiful, you have a flat ass". And she thought to herself; "Ugh! Men, unprovoked, are trash".

So, now she goes around referring to this masculine Being as "Trash", but can you blame her though? I wouldn't. I mean, she's been hurt by this Being, he's put her through hell, he's done horrible and unimaginable things that no human in their right state of mind could ever do. He wasn't loyal, he stole from her, he wasn't reliable, he made her feel insecure, he did not live up to her expectations of him (ones that he created), the same man who begged her to be with him and promised to protect her heart, although she may have refused his proposal at first, she eventually caved in, and he scarred her, and now look where she's ended? She has lost all trust and respect for all men. And don't get me wrong, no one can be excused for acting out because of what someone has done to them in the past.

Remember: "Everything we do in life is a choice." And so, if you choose to hurt others because you have been hurt before; you are no different from the person who has hurt you.

One thing I want to say about this Feminal Being though, is that; it's not that she isn't aware of the obvious fact that it is not all men who do not know how to behave like decent human beings, that it isn't all men who are violent, abusive and/or immature, it was just an unfortunate event for her to have met the wrong ones, or rather ones that had not evolved to their highest level of human decency, but they sure have taught her a lot. A lot about herself and about self-love, a lot on how to rely on God's love & strength, because that's the one man who could never break her heart. They have taught her to be independent while being interdependent with those around her, to value herself, and to understand her worth, to respect herself enough to walk away from situations that do not serve her highest self, and to continue to pour all of that love she seeks to pour into others, right into her cup, till there's an overflow from her side, that were she to give to another, she wouldn't be left with a sense of depletion because she would not be giving from a place of nothingness, but rather from a place of wholeness. She has come to learn that for her, being with a man will not be out of desperation for love, it will not be as a result of her loneliness, no! It will be because she is seeking a life partner, her equal to build with, not because she's incapable of building alone, but because two are better than one. But remember, romantic love is not a requisite for everyone in the world, it is a choice for those who have urges and desires and do not wish to be alone.

However, don't get me wrong, because on most days I want to scream from the top of my lungs; ALL MEN ARE "TRASH", which is a notion used around to describe a male specie who violates, diminishes, traumatizes, and just doesn't show a woman any respect. But a part of me chokes from my own voice because I am not so biased. I used to hate it so much when people were sexually assaulted, heartbroken, or abused by a man and they would come out and declare that really, "MEN ARE TRASH". I always just felt like they were always just feeling sorry for themselves as the victim, playing the victim-card and wanting to be pitied but never wanted to expose or find out the true reasons behind why the perpetrator did it, whether they were struggling with something that needed to be dealt with, the root cause, or what. Because the way a person treats you, stems from how they feel deep within themselves, and while both sides are important- the victim's and the perpetrator's, looking at the number of assaults against women by men, I do not know however, if I feel the same way as before. I know someone else's behaviour or actions towards you shouldn't deter or alter your beliefs and the way that you view life holistically, but if I'm being entirely honest; looking at the number of women who have been hurt by men, be it physically or emotionally, judging from my own personal experiences too, I fail to look at all the men the same way that I used to before, and that is with respect. I just feel as though every guy is now out there trying to get "it", that that is the only thing men want from the Female Specie. I somehow feel it's what gives them a sense of power and control, because it leaves us lifeless and weak, being assaulted or broken, that is. However, that does not mean that I have written off every single gent from my list of potentials, because I genuinely respect everyone until they give me a reason not to, and also because I am such a hopeless romantic; I want a man, I want to be wife'd up and babied, I want someone I can call daddy(and no, I do not have any daddy issues, it's just cute, okay?), I would like to wake up close to a masculine Being and go to bed on his chest like the South African Xhosa tribe would call it 'Esifubeni sendoda', someone I can spend the rest of my days with, I crave that, the partnership, and doing this life thing with someone right by my side, I want that. But also, if that never happens, then I would still be okay. However, if it does happen that I find a life partner, and it so happens that I do have sons with them, I would make it my mission to let my sons believe and know that it is wrong; initiating an act that is as horrendous as rape, physical and emotional abuse, without the consent of the other party is wrong, and that it has consequences, thus they will be held accountable and responsible for their actions. That hurting a woman, let alone anyone does not make them strong but only weak, because it mirrors the issues that lie deep within them, their own insecurities, and struggles.

Well, that boils down to my next point, that maybe men are struggling in silence? They may be afraid of Vulnerability? Maybe they do not want to be seen as weak and so, they hide away their pain & struggles and can't even open up about what it is that makes them act the way they do towards women? They act all tough and manly-like but really all they need is someone willing to listen and not judge? (I could be wrong though) but here's my take on this:

The mental state of a person is what makes them act the way that they do. It all starts in the mind. It all starts within. And maybe, just maybe men are struggling with the issue of pornography? That maybe when they see women all they can think of is having a piece of that? Because their mind has been contaminated with what's evil, and because it's addictive, it has a stronghold on them that they want the experience for themselves, "maybe the screen just isn't enough", or maybe there's more to this than just that, and but what does that lead to? – Abuse, Rape, Murder, Kidnappings of young kids, Molestation of infants, and infidelity in relationships. Perhaps the issue is not just pornography? The issue may be that they were once molested and exposed to such behaviour at a young age? Or maybe the issue is in the conversations that men hold when they have gathered around? Perhaps the issue is the peer pressure of "how are you past this age and still haven't had sex yet? You have to get it with someone to fit in dude!!", or maybe the issue is that when he was a young boy his uncles or father used to shout at him for not being man enough, so he felt compelled to try and prove a point that he's a man? And the only depiction of a man he was ever exposed to was "someone who beats up a woman, someone who gets what they want their way, forcefully, someone who looks down on women because he is superior, and the alpha male and the woman must bow down to him. Someone who drinks, and smokes." And that could be because maybe being addicted to drugs numbs the pain or shame, maybe being drunk takes away the reality of life and having to be a man, a leader? I mean, after all, that is what men were taught when growing up, that they have to be the head of the house, and I'm in no way saying that women cannot be leaders because a woman is very much capable of leading.

Then again, maybe men have this void so deep within that remains unfilled, so they think forcefully having sex with someone i.e.

Raping them, is a way of "giving love in hopes of it being reciprocated"? And that is absolutely wrong! And maybe men just want to feel a love so gentle and not so demanding, a love so understanding of their imperfections and flaws, but can't get that? Maybe men do feel the way that women do, the same way a woman wants to feel loved by this other gender, the same way a woman wants to be validated by this Masculine Being, the same way a woman seeks attention and affection from this male specie, maybe, just maybe he wants the same? But he's got all of this pressure coming at him, he's got to be the provider, he's got to be the Head of the house, he has got to be the strong one because everyone in the family is looking up to him, he's got to find a stable job with a stable income so that he may be able to feed every single mouth that's depending on him to provide, that he rarely gets the time to just feel? But then again, without disregarding the male species first instinct of "having to be the provider and the strongest", times have changed and are continuously changing and so, as much as it feels like men should carry all this weight alone, more and more women are becoming independent and maybe that threatens men? Because they feel as though women have so much already and the only thing that they have is a sense of power, of being in control of things, thus having women become so independent strips them of their power? But only an individual who isn't evolved enough will yield to that perception.

But then again, I am not saying catcalling or infidelity is right, let alone murder, rape, and abuse. None of these actions should be justified. It's disgusting! It's intolerable! It's infuriating! So agitating!!! But can we also start focusing on the root cause and not just the victim? Every woman or man who has ever been raped, killed, abused, or been through the trauma all because of another Being deserves the grief, they deserve our condolences. They deserve our empathy, they deserve to be believed when they speak out about any form of violence against them, and they deserve justice. They deserve their peace again; they deserve the restoration of their Dignity. But how are we going to stop this if it keeps recurring and every time it happens, we are aggressive about it? We point fingers, we wage war against the flesh and not the spirit? This (the abuse, the lies, the cheating, the assaults) that is happening right here, right now, has happened before, what are we going to do differently? Are we going to keep complaining on social media whenever it happens and just wait for the next victim? Or are we going to do something? Words without actions are just that – words. Are we going to report the case to the criminal justice system and have them lock the "problem" away without dealing with the root cause? Or are we going to start educating young men(boys) on how to treat a woman? Are we going to encourage Men to go counselling on the issues that our men face mentally, emotionally, or spiritually but are too ashamed to open up about, all in the name of "mele uQine, uyindoda" (you must be strong because you're a man)?

A tree is never dead until you have cut deep into the roots and have made sure that it is completely dead. Maybe if the root of all this evil was being attacked, there wouldn't be a next victim, maybe that girl, woman, boy, even that granny sitting at home scared and wondering 'who's next?', will not walk in the fear of "what if I'm next?", that's if we got to the root of it all.

Most actions that people perpetrate are as a result of how they feel, and sometimes it is something that lies way beneath the surface, so, were we to only judge the action and not the root cause, we would not have dealt with the problem at all.

Which brings me to my next point; Maybe we need to start questioning what is out of balance within them, to understand why they keep doing it, and not just what was done, who did it, and to whom it was done. At the end of the day, we all play party in such situations, be it cheating, abuse, rape, etc., thus it is only fit for each of us to take responsibility for our own actions, take the lessons that come, heal the situation and ourselves in the best way that we possibly can, and become better, instead of being bitter, sad, and holding onto grudges for the whole of eternity.

CHAPTER 3- A DOSE OF MASCULINITY

Masculinity is a very touchy topic to speak on, given that there are so many misconceptions about what it means to be a man, and that has all been imposed by society, and of course, you and I both form part of society.

Men, what a specie!

Men have always been considered a strong force. Their strength derived from mostly their physical abilities. Men have always been considered the masculine Beings, masculine in their physicality. Men have always been considered breadwinners, the providers in their households, the leaders! They always have been considered the sexual beings, or should I say the "thirsters of sex". But some men are experiencing a spiritual attack and an identity crisis, whether they realize it or not. An attack of power and that of sexuality. It feels burdensome to not be working as a man, to not have your whole life figured out at a particular age because, to be honest, men's worth has always been measured based on their financial status or stability. Men have always experienced the pressure of having to succeed at an earlier stage in life to prove their manliness; If you can make money and are able to care for your family, you will receive recognition and respect. I am not saying to men "go out there and be lazy", because that would be careless of me, every individual must have a sense of direction on their own, whether it be a man or a woman, but men should not feel as though their worth is defined in terms of or derived from monetary value. "You are human before you are anything else." That means that you have feelings and emotions, you are not just a robotic structure constantly working with no time to get in touch with your emotions and/or feelings. And even with my awareness that a man is more practical and a woman, the more emotional Being, you too require love and affection, you require time out just to feel and to be felt. Now, before I get too deep into this topic, allow me to go back to what masculinity has always been defined as.

Masculinity is a very tricky topic to poke one's nose into, as I have already mentioned, but I'll take that chance.

Men were always made to care for women, from the very moment a man realized that a woman is bone of his bone; his pillar and flesh of his flesh; his structure, the man knew that he just had to care for and protect his woman.

But it wasn't until there was a shift in the atmosphere that the Male began to act the total opposite from what his initial task was to the Female. The Male had forgotten his purpose of caring for and protecting His Female, and perhaps that was because he found it difficult to forgive because he was so conformed to keeping things within and not releasing, so he began to exhibit violence towards her, it was cruel, his actions towards her. He turned bitter, began to look out for only himself. Selfish, he became. He wanted it all for himself, the riches, the wealth, he did not want to share any of it unless there was something in return, he was to gain. And knowing the Male, he has always been considered the sexual

Being, he is as thirsty as they come, and so he used that element of his character to his advantage. He thought to himself; "If the Female wants to survive in this life, she has to make it through me, I know her weak spots, after all, she was woven from me, she needs me to provide for her, to cater to her needs" therefore, I will offer her a helping hand but will use that only to gain pleasure from her, I will make sure that I reach the uppermost level in the ranking of wealth to ensure that were she ever to need anything, she would run to me. Nonetheless, one thing that the Male could not deny or fight with; was the fact that because the Female was woven from him, she too had the abilities that he had, if not more, so she was more than capable of surviving on her own, she was more than capable of providing for herself, but because the flow of life was created in such a way that both the Male and Female have to coexist with each other, utilizing all their vigorousness, intelligence, tenderness, faults, differences and blending all those together to bring about an extension to what is referred to as the population, men and women had to reach a point of realization that they needed each other after all.

If you will, allow me to tap just a tad bit on what a Spiritual attack is without going too deep into such a matter.

A spiritual attack is an attack, be it physically or psychologically by the ruler of the dark forces in the spiritual realm and on the face of the earth, through the use of supernatural powers, to cause harm to a targeted individual who does not believe in or serve the ruler of the dark forces.

But remember; not everything wrong or bad that you experience or go through as you journey through life is a spiritual attack, some are lessons to be learned from, which ultimately lead to your strengthening and growth, whereas others are actually weapons, bondages, or curses that need to be renounced.

Now, let us talk about money, shall we? I'll start off by quoting the famous Bible verse on money; "the love of Money is the root of all kinds of evil". Funny how you know this quote but fail to realize that it's playing out right at this moment.

Money, a noun, that is. It is a means of exchange. Money is the key to accessing wealth, respect, and any materialistic thing you can think of. Everyone is chasing money, chasing what is referred to as "the bag", and as innocent as it seems sometimes to joke around about wanting to make money, loads and loads of it, one needs to be careful that they aren't driven by the forces and their hunger, and/or desperation for money. Not having money can be depressive, especially in the era that we are living in right now where money is so important if you want to maintain that lux lifestyle, but also seems to be a need for the average person who is just trying to get through life on a daily. Money, as I have already mentioned, is a means of exchange and without it, it has become very challenging to survive. Money has become a necessity because to access one's needs, like basic food stuff, clothing, and shelter, one needs to at least have some form of money to be granted access to all of that. Without money, you are most likely to be homeless, foodless, and useless, well at least that's how you or others will perceive yourself, unless you have relatives who take care of you financially, if so, you need to consider yourself privileged.

To top up what I have just said about money; money denotes value, but in today's terms, it is not just monetary value, it is a measure of one's worth. If you are a monied individual, then you are most likely to be respected or to be held in high regard, but if you have no cent to your name, people will not miss the chance of disrespecting you at any second. Your opinions, no matter how valid or accurate, will not even be considered, just because you don't have "a money". What ever happened to respecting everyone, regardless of their age, gender, or status? When it comes to financial status, having a high-profile status in terms of your finances will get you places. Kids from rich families who aren't so bright academically can access the best education from our education system, through hiring tutors, to paying their way up to receive a pass on their report card, or to gain access to an admission letter at the University. Truth is; money is associated with a lot of good and bad things, from the accessibility of one's needs, to travelling the world, affording a luxurious lifestyle, corruption from government officials and bribery to traffic officers, money can be a scandalous scheme. People are willing to go the extra mile just to make "a money", but is it really worth it though? Not to mistaken me for sounding like I am not a liker of money or fine things, no! In fact, I love money, I mean, who doesn't? There are just so many things I can do with money, like ticking off that vacation or solo cation on my bucket list, to buying an apartment or spending money on a brand new car, not to forget the items of clothing I would buy for myself, I want to travel the world, of course, I too want "a money", I crave the soft life, I do not for a second want to believe that I was made to be poor, I was created to experience abundance in every form, however, I do not over obsess about money, because money isn't the only form or measure of abundance, and money being one's driving force can cause a lot of damage, not to just to oneself, but to so many other people.

Money will make you want to overstep boundaries, ditch your values, ethics, or morals, just for the sake of having more. But what is money if not the fluidity of exchange rates from one hand to the next? Money has always been associated with success, whereas success is associated with having power, being on top, hence, if you have "a money", you are considered one of the top dogs in this game of life, but if you don't have money, you are considered a lowlife.

You are probably wondering why I am so focused on the topic of money under the heading of "masculinity". Well, to put you at ease, allow me to explain myself.

See, as mentioned before, men have always been considered as the providers of their families, their responsibility was always that they have to find a job, go to work, work their butts off, make money, use the money to purchase anything that was needed back at home. Thus, money is an important factor in being a man. By the same token, money is becoming more and more of a negative influence on the character of most men.

Let's take a look at some of the horrendous activities that are being perpetrated on some of our young girls; starting off with kidnappings of young girls as a way of human trafficking, to be sold on the market as sex slaves. Butchering of young girls and even older women, only to take a part of their body to be used for rituals in some quick get rich scheme, and with no proof to back this up, I would like to think that some of these schemes could most probably include sleeping with the opposite gender, let alone the same-sex, as a way to get even richer, but is it all worth it, to go to such extreme measures only for a momentary pleasure?

But then again, I do not want to put the blame on just one specific party, make it seem as if men are the only ones with a motive to only make money because see, there are men who tend to think that the only thing women want is money or financial stability, and these are men who probably have been in a nasty situation before, where a woman was just hungry for paper and only used the man for his money because such women exist, materialistically driven women who just want all things money, but the sad part is that the men who have experienced that trauma cannot unsee every other woman as such, even though they aren't. At the same time, such men(those who see women as only seeking financial stability) are men who, they, themselves only have that to offer, and nothing more, so, no emotional stability, no spiritual maturity, just the provision of money, which is sad, because relationships require more than just that, what will be left of a relationship that is centred around money, when there is no longer any? And the same principle applies to a woman who feels as though women are only sought after for the sake of being offered financial stability by men, some men can offer you more than just money, these are the kind of gents who will stick with you even when it gets tough and when those financially loaded men dump you like a hot potato. Women who can take care of themselves but still want a man by their side as a life partner, do very much exist, and not all financially stable men just want to use you for a price. Truth is we have all had a little twist to our views, as a result of our past experiences that have left us feeling a little bitter and guarded, and we have had to take a lesson or two from. We can no longer see things with a fresh new perspective because we are always going to be a little too guarded, what if she hurts me? What if he breaks me? That fear has brought our trust to a nadir and it's sad.

Most men struggle to see their identity outside of financial wealth. So, if a man is financially unstable, meaning not having the necessary financial means to provide for and care for his loved ones, or himself, he is most likely to fall into a depressive state, because his identity has always been centred around materialism. Women on the other hand do not often experience this issue, although I am pretty much aware of the fact that more and more women are 'woke' these days and are becoming more independent, chasing their dreams and goals, however, the pain of not having money will always hit different between a man and a woman, because with a woman, marriage, and the ability to have babies was always considered a woman's trophy or number one prize.

Your bank balance does not define your masculinity, neither does your job title. Your having to be aggressive to prove your manhood because "men do not take nonsense from anybody" is not what makes you a man, you not shedding tears and having to hide away your failures and struggles all in the name of "men don't cry, the strength of a man is never to be emotional" is not what masculinity is.

The standards that "society" has set for men are what has ruined the concept of masculinity, it is so easy to notice the wrongs that society has imposed on women and try to correct that, while ignoring the construed view society has placed on the concept of masculinity. Women have experienced suppression in all different kind of ways, while men "seemed" to have had it easy, but have you taken a greater look at how difficult it must have been for a man to have his emotions suppressed because only women were given the freedom or liberation to fully express themselves? And who denied them this freedom, you ask? Probably themselves, but my point is any form of emotional build-up in a person is unhealthy, so imagine the build-up inside of a man of all the repressed emotions and feelings of shame, failure, lack, loss, inability, and trauma because of his pride, ego, and lack of knowledge that it is okay to tap into both your masculine and feminine energies, I mean, that must be terrible!

Nonetheless, one thing to note about men is that they are very visual, which is something you have heard before, and because men are visual, it makes them sexual. Because men are sexual beings by nature, they tend to experience an attack more often on their sexuality, I know it sounds like I am trying to excuse most men's behaviour of cheating, assaulting, lying, or having affairs outside of their original commitments i.e., infidelity, but that is not what is happening right here, you just need to continue reading through to get to where I am trying to go with this point. Allow me to dive in a little on this topic of visuality and men, however, as you read through, just remember that I am no scientist or medical professional; so any diagnosis of how men's brains are wired, is based on research that has been proven in the past and published for the public to read.

Going back to my point of males being sexual and visual, Males are known progenitors, and of course, procreation exists as a result of a sexual union between both the male and female specie, but men are considered the "carriers of the seeds", hence, they are prone to wanting sex more than the female specie. The male specie naturally has that urge to penetrate a woman at any given time, they are always ready to plant, whereas it may take a while for the female specie to get into the groove, the female has to prepare herself every month for the fertilization of the ground (her ovaries and uterus/womb) to be able to carry the seed from a male, but what stops most men from fulfilling/satisfying or giving into that urge, is self-control. So, men who lack that control over themselves when the urge comes are most likely to commit rape, any form of sexual assault, or anything disturbing like cheating/infidelity etc. Take it like this; a water tank is always carrying water, I know it's not in all cases but just take this example as is and stop trying to think outside of the box *jokes, but let's just stick to this scenario so as to get to the point that I am trying to get across. So, back to the example; a water tank is always carrying water, the water goes out through the tap, but it isn't always that you will find the tap running down with water, no! The tap is always closed, the only time where you will find the tap running with water is when there is a need for the use of water, for example, when there is a need to cook food, water is essential, when there is a need to bath, and when there is also a need to quench that thirst.

The same applies to men, you are the carriers of seeds, but just because you carry seeds, it does not mean that you constantly have to plant seed everywhere you go, or all the time, no! And I know what you are probably thinking to yourself right now; 'so is she saying that the only time I need to open the tap i.e., "have sex" is when I want to make a baby?' and the answer to that silly question of yours, is no. Now, I have a chapter dedicated to the topic of sex, so I know that that will ease your frustration with regards to the statement I have just made above, but for now, what I can tell you is that sex is not just about reproduction, it is very much also meant for pleasure, but it will have to depend on the kind of definition you attach to pleasure.

So, this all boils down to the closing of the tap, which in real terms I will refer to as "self-control". What is self-control? Self-control is the ability to tame oneself against acting on one's desires or emotions when faced with challenging situations, this can be emotions arising due to conflicts, or offences, or can be because of desires from temptations.

The issue with Rape is an inner struggle for men. I am aware that molestation and sexual assault (any kind) does not only happen to women, and that it happens to men too because women rape too, but the perpetrators of such acts are mostly men, which is what my focus will be on.

The world as we live in it and know it, is filled with so much love, peace, and/or harmony, but balancing it out is also hatred, wars or conflicts, and most commonly temptation. Temptation is an urge, often strong, to do something that one knows will have negative consequences in return or if one acts upon it. The test of self-control lies in temptation. You cannot say you are a strong individual if you have never been faced with challenges that were meant to break you or pull you down but have built you up instead. The same principle applies to self-control, you cannot say you have self-discipline if you have never experienced an urge so strong, yet so wrong, but you did not give in to it. A lot of crimes and violations against the human species are due to desires, messed up ones; a desire to own a beautiful car, but do not have the money to purchase one, so how about I "take"(which is a more pleasant way of saying 'steal') that car parked on the side of the road with no driver inside, locked, but I'll go the extra mile of learning how to break into a car, start the ignition without a key, well some cars don't need keys anyways, spot a tracker on a car, remove the tracker, and get new plates, but before attempting to do all of that, a police officer walks past the car I am about to 'take', but I will not be deterred from my mission, that is just a distraction and an attempt to try to scare me off, but I will not give into that nudge feeling in my heart space to not continue with the execution of my plan, as I walk to the car to take it.

Choices, so many times we are presented with these, and the opportunities to truly choose the right one. Whenever you experience temptation, it is not that you will not be presented with a choice to choose otherwise, you always will be presented with one, but it all boils down to how strong enough you are to resist that temptation. Self-control, also known as self-discipline, is a form of strength. So, yes, men have always been considered strong in their physicality, how well they are built, but how strong are men emotionally? The strength in self-discipline is an emotional one, and not necessarily a physical one, the war between the fulfilment of an urge and the suppression of the emotions to act upon that urge, is an internal one, so before you even carry out the act of fulfilling your urge, you would have first had an internal conflict, which, in a more sophisticated English language; is referred to as an intrapersonal conflict, the conflict between an individual and themselves, a conflict within a person. And if we were to be entirely honest, based on the numbers, in this case, the statistics of rape, domestic violence, and cheating, it is evident that men have a weakness when it comes to exercising their self-control, or that women are great masterminds who have never been caught. If you are a man reading this, you are probably saying to yourself 'that is utter rubbish, the only reason most rape and domestic violence cases are of women and are initiated by men, is because men do not report these violations against themselves when they experience them' and you know what, you are right, absolutely correct! But my point is not utter nonsense, because the sad truth is that even if men were to report the cases of rape, not to say that women do not rape, but the perpetrator would most likely turn out to be a man, or the numbers wouldn't be as high, so my point of "men are struggling with the weakness of indiscipline" still stands. But one important factor to remember in all of this is that "it is not all men", but rather the vast majority of men.

It must be confusing for a man being told the words "there's no need to feel insecure because a woman is making more money than you, or is in a higher position than you", which I agree with, there's absolutely no need to feel less of a man because a woman earns more money than you, but it is not so easy for a man to not feel insecure about that when there are more and more women who are becoming "independent", acting as if they don't need men, which is false, see, the major reason women are defensive and cold towards men is that they have had terrible experiences in the past and instead of choosing to release the anger and pain, and learn the lesson, they have held onto it because they keep encountering the same man, just in a different body and with a different name. After all, men refuse to change their behaviour all in the name of "this is how men are wired to act".

As mentioned already, men are natural born providers, whereas women on the other hand are naturally nurturers, that is the balance that the Creator created for both men and women. I know women are often celebrated for being able to birth life, but let's not act as though it is only the women who are special in this case, because men are special too. The male carries seed, he provides the seed which is the beginning of a life, which is later transferred into the field of a woman, and once the seed has found fertile ground to latch onto, it then leads to the woman, in turn, becoming the incubator of the human life, and I would like to believe that the reason why the woman has been gifted with the ability or gift of incubation of the human race, is that the female is prone to being more of a nurturer and the male more, of a provider, and of course, the whole process of human creation in the female body is such a beautiful, amazing thing to experience, it is very awing, but never fail to remember that both men and women play an important role, they just play different roles in procreation, but that does not make either one of them less important.

But one true thing about men is that men need to stop shying away from taking responsibility and holding themselves accountable for their actions because the truth is a man would rather blatantly tell a white lie in front of a woman's face than acknowledge that he lost his self-control when he went out to cheat on her with another woman. As a person, you need to acknowledge your weaknesses and stop acting as though you are a victim, in fact, a man would rather play the victim card and blame the "other woman" for tempting him to have sex with her, or for leading him to not break a connection with her, while he was the one who initiated the connection to begin with, and for some reason that makes me begin to question whether Adam was tempted by Eve to eat the apple, or if he was the one who was tempted by the serpent and convinced Eve to eat the fruit from the forbidden tree of life and lied to the Creator about Eve being the one who convinced him to eat the fruit, because more and more men these days are becoming conniving, cunning liars, but let me break the previous scenario down for you; As a man you knew you were in a relationship with someone, whether the two of you had labels or not, and if there were no labels or an actual commitment, then that says a lot about you, how dare you awaken a woman's love with no intention of loving her? In my world, we call gents like you cowards, that "I'm just here for a good time not a long time" type of guy, yeah playa! A man who disturbs a woman's peace has his own internal turmoil, and so, you led her on, this lady, but wanted "no strings attached" and when you finally met the woman you wanted to commit to, the one you wanted to wife up, you ended up playing them both, because here you were with what you call an "obstacle" which wouldn't make way for you to treat right the girl you finally felt magic with, and so you felt stuck and what felt right to do at the moment was to lie to your one, telling her half-truths and making her feel crazy every single time she felt compelled and tried to confront you about your "other woman" when you knew all along that it was her intuition signalling to her that you were just bluffing on her, but why? Why couldn't you have just been honest with everyone from the start? That is what is puzzling, because if you truly did fall short or had a moment of weakness I believe that your one would have been understanding, maybe not at the exact moment that you would have told her, but eventually, because I believe that she knows and understands that as humans, none of us are perfect and I don't think anyone expects you to be, you just have to be real with yourself and every time that you fall short to temptation, you don't stay down, you get up and keep trying, trying to say no, and show that you are willing to do better the next time you are presented with the same or similar challenge, because at the end of the day if you are honest about your shortcomings and are willing to change and are actively working towards that change, no one can deny you that chance because you would have already awarded yourself that chance, and if you truly didn't want this other woman then you would have let her know in the beginning before you tried to establish a relationship with someone else, instead of trying to be the little ghost on the 1995 film titled Casper, or Dora the explorer?

CHAPTER 4- THE STEREOTYPE IS REAL

Growing up in a household with boys and being a girl child was challenging, challenging in the sense that my mother did not allow me the freedom to wear whatever I wanted to, especially when it came to anything that was considered "too revealing". Both my sister and I could not walk around wearing shorts or any skirt that was considered way too above our knees regardless of how hot the temperature was, whenever my brothers or father were around the house. And well, I did not really have a problem with that because I, myself did not enjoy wearing short stuff or perhaps my dislike of short pairs of clothing was born from the rules that were set for me? But my issue came in when my brothers would walk around the house with no top on and it was considered okay, because "well, it is very hot today". I always felt that it was a little unfair that as a female child I was not allowed to roam around the house wearing "revealing pairs of clothing", whereas my mother seemed to not have a problem with the half-nakedness of my brothers.

But it has occurred to me, just like it has to many, that male privilege exists. And although it might not exist for every male figure out there, it does exist for most men. I remember how it was growing up, I'd do most of the cleaning with my mother and sister, whilst my father and brothers would just be sitting around. We would then proceed to do the cooking and dishwashing, and on the weekends, we would usually do the laundry. I was always annoyed at how my brothers never helped. They would only help when, like in the shopping stores on the intercom, it had been announced that their help was required, and then, and only then, would they see it fit to help.

To this day I wonder if my brothers and father were just portraying their male instincts to come off as leaders by not helping around the house, I wonder if they felt a sense of "being in charge" when my mother, sister and I were the only ones who would do the work around the house. Perhaps it gave them a sense of "being in control", or some form of power over us? Because for them, domestic work is for the female species? Although they would still use the very same dishes we had washed, to dish out food for themselves that they hadn't prepared, just because they were hungry. However, it never occurred to them once, that they were going to need to use the same dishes the next time they wanted to dish out food, perhaps the plates were miraculously going to be clean the next time they needed to use them? And the food, like manna, was going to fall from heaven, and miraculously appear right before them? Well, if that is how you were raised, with the mindset that only women are conditioned to do the domestic work around the house, sorry to burst your bubble, but cleaning, cooking, and any other chore that relates to domestic work is a basic life skill that everyone needs, to survive, not just women. Wake up, it's the 21st century for crying out loud, some old methods and ways of doing things will not work or apply in this new lifetime. It sounds like an attack on men, I know, but see, I have nothing against men but this stereotype of women being the individuals that need to do the domestic work around the house without the help of the other gender makes me sick to my stomach. And it is something that I feel I will never understand.

I believe when God created a helper i.e., Eve for Adam, he didn't necessarily mean a slave or a maid, because of what he added onto that, regarding authority. He, in no way, was only referring to Adam but to both Beings He had created, because how can a maid or slave have the same dominion and/or power as his master? I do not know what more evidence men require to prove that they are equals to women who carry the same amount of authority and dominion as them.

Gender stereotype has been an ongoing issue that we have been struggling with as nations. So, allow me to explain exactly what that is in the best possible way that I can, and not just touch base on it.

Gender stereotype is derived from what is referred to as "gender role", and what that entails is; the acceptable or appropriate behaviours and attitudes of an individual, based on their sex or in other terms, gender. In layman terms, that means that if you were born a female, then there is a particular way in which you need to act and do things, for example, females have always been presumed to be the ones responsible for most or well, all of the domestic work in a household, females were considered to always present themselves in a way that was acceptable to society and that meant to always look tidy, not just referring to themselves or their physical appearances, but their homes as well, and honestly, that wasn't too bad of a standard but the interesting part for me has got to be how females were limited in their capacities, or capabilities. No offence to any housewife(housewives aren't just domesticated women who have no life, some of these women have their own businesses to run), but this may come off as offensive, okay? Women were considered just, "woven from a man", so I, as a man, had the power and control over you, you were my possession, valuable? Well, not in all cases. Men expected women to submit to them whenever and however they liked, "they" referring to the men. I know how it may seem as though I am generalising, but just keep in mind, 'it is not all men'.

As a young girl, you just had to know that growing up, everything that your mother was teaching you was just preparation for your 'wifely duties' to your husband one day. The duties of a woman as a wife were to take care of everyone and everything in her household. A typical day of a woman back in the day would be to wake up, cook for her husband, that would be before the kids were born, to ensure that the house was clean, and of course, to make babies. The man would go out to till the fields and tend the animals and that all just seemed fair and just at the time, and it worked well for the people who lived through that era, no judgement. But with time came new developments, and with new developments came new passions for things, for instance; engineers were needed in such developments, architectures too, then new business developments were established which required business managers in handling the operations of the organisations, accountants in managing and making sound decisions regarding the finances of the business, and with such developments came illnesses, diseases and disorders that required proper medical attention thus doctors, nurses, pharmacists and therapists became a necessity, educators too, were needed to educate on such developments and impart skills that would be necessary in knowing how to manage such developments etc. With such developments and expansions, things that were once considered just hobbies or just normal activities that were part of the daily lives of humans, became passions for many, for instance, the production of artsy products, cooking, taking care of babies and people. Many became very passionate about all these things which, over time, were considered occupations for most and became part of the human race's living.

Even with such developments, women were not seen beyond just being domesticated, and honestly, that was suppression. Women have always been a powerful force on their own, and the suppression only came from those who could not acknowledge and accept change. See, because women had for a very long time, been considered to be domesticated and only that, there was a fear to accept change from both the women and the men. But the very first woman who(I unfortunately do not know, but must have existed at the time, and whom we as women owe thanks to for being brave enough to embrace the change and grab the opportunities that were presented to her with both hands), stepped up to the plate, with the fear in her chest, and lump in her throat, and said no to the suppression, which simply began the movement that many call feminism, but in essence is just a call for equality between both genders, and that has changed the narrative. Equality is fairness, it is treating all parties involved without discrimination, equality is offering all parties the freedom of expression in their individuality, it is being just in one's treatment towards, well, in this case, both genders.

In the previous chapter, I spoke about identity crisis, how most men are currently experiencing that. A lot of hatred and abuse from men stems from fear and fear from a lack. Men have always known their responsibility to be to provide for their families or loved ones, and so when that role is stripped off of them, they feel that they have no other role to fulfil or just nothing left of them. And when that is the case, there will be a sense of hatred developed towards women like, how come she gets to be a mother, have the ability or superpower rather, to birth a human and still get to graduate from College or University, get to be employed, let alone own her own business, or businesses?

I say some men are currently faced with an identity crisis because for so long men have always been identified as the successful ones. From the beginning of one's existence, one has an assignment they have been assigned to, a vision they must see-through, a purpose intended for them, and as much as some basic household chores like domestic work, have turned into actual jobs as more and more people are getting busier and need a helping hand around the house, they do still remain a basic chore for each human to do, allow me to explain further; washing dishes, cleaning the house, cooking, doing laundry, etc., it's all the same as peeing, taking a dunk (excuse the language), eating, and sleeping, these are all activities that are part of our daily routine which make everything in our lives function properly. For you to do work and perform well the next day, you need to rest, you need the energy, hence you need food for all those vitamins, proteins, and stamina, but requiring someone else to make the food for you is a little absurd because you are the one who needs the food, yes, they do too but as a human which is what I am before I am categorised as a woman or a man, I can appreciate splitting the chores in half or just having a helping hand. If I do the cooking can you at least do the dishes? And if I do the cleaning can you at least throw the laundry into the washing machine, like, am I asking too much? Asking you to wash the dishes that you ate in, and are going to need for the next meal (mine included)? Asking you to wash your laundry (mine included)? Is that too much to ask? Men who feel that domestic work is for women alone are lazy, that's just that on that, I can understand that we weren't all raised the same, perhaps you were raised in a household where you had your mother, sisters, or aunties doing all the chores around the house for you, that does not mean that you should not learn how to do the chores yourself. If your aunties or mother weren't there to cook, clean, and tidy up the house, who would have to do it? If you are being honest with me and yourself, if you were staying in a bachelor apartment on your own with no one there to assist you, who was going to cook for you? Who was going to clean the apartment? Who was going to do your laundry? Who was going to wash the very same dishes you ate from, was it not going to be you?(Unless of course you'd hire a maid to come do all of that for you). But my point is; if you are a man or a woman who does not take initiative when it comes to domestic-related work, you are just lazy. Do you see that? But I understand where this all stems from, it is a part of our history, that is how things have always been, that is how our mothers and their mothers were raised, to slave around for men, in fact, then it wasn't seen as slavery, it was normal. However, times have changed, interesting how you will find a man saying "I will not marry a broke woman" but would still expect the same woman to go to work, return home and still do chores, while he does what, Chill with the boys? Sometimes I cannot help but wonder if these developments ruined the intended flow of life? Don't get me wrong, I love change, I embrace it and I am very open to it, but I can't help but wonder if the developments that have taken place over the years have taken away the very essence or meaning of life, to just live and breathe? But then again, life would be too basic without evolution and change, we were created with brilliance, imagination, and skill, how could we ever let that go to waste?

Let me introduce a few individuals to this show called The Battle of The Genders. The first on my list is the 'Masculine Masculinity', first thing you notice about this gent is that he is a man. Now, you can see that in his physical features, he is well built, in his genitals, he has a full-on beard, he has that deep vibrational bass voice to him when he becomes vocal. Our second contestant on the show will be the 'Feminine Femininity', she is the opposite of the Masculine Masculinity, she, on the other hand, has a more petite body shape compared to him and speaks rather softly and is just sweet in all that she is. These are the standards that most people expect from women and men. But allow me to introduce you to two other contestants, the Masculine Femininity and Feminine Masculinity. The Feminine Masculinity is a man, that is the first thing I need you to notice about him. He is however not as aggressive as the Masculine Masculinity. He is a bit soft; he allows himself to get emotional when needs be, unlike some parts of the

47

Masculine Masculinity who believes that crying is for the weak. He is not too over dominant and believes in embracing both sides of femininity and masculinity, and the same applies to the Masculine Femininity, she is soft, but she knows how to toughen up. Life is all about balance, and as an individual, you need to somewhat embrace both sides to you, the emotional and practical side that is.

The truth about stereotype is that it puts rather unrealistic standards towards how men and women should act, behave, and look. As a human race, we have been created with different personalities, different features, different thought processes, different tastes to style, music, and food(although theses can develop/be influenced according to the environment in which you were raised), but expecting the participants of a particular gender to act the same way is super unrealistic.

The likeness of God is the alignment to his will, one purpose, and the oneness with God, it is not necessarily about the physical appearance, it has nothing to do with the exterior.

Personally, I think that most women are operating from a place of pain, disappointment, and fear. Of course, no man is perfect, nobody is, not all men are good guys, some men are douchebags, some men operate from a place of darkness, which is reflected through their actions and behaviour, but the reason why I say that most women(and men too), are operating from a place of pain, disappointment, and fear, is because they have been hurt before, they have had a man who caused them so much grief, brought them to their lowest point(not only in a romantic sense), these women have been disappointed before, they have had moments where they naively put their trust in a man, of which they probably should not have in the first place, but love can make you selflessly want to give up yourself for someone else, ad let's not forget how gullible and trusting women can be, however, what did that do? It got them burnt, which ultimately has led them to operate from a place of fear. These women are scared, 'what if he turns out to be exactly like how the previous guy was? What if he also bruises my heart? Are his sweet, sweet words and kind gestures towards me just another facade ready to explode into disappointment?' Therefore, because of that fear, I will put my guard up, I am not going to easily trust a man, I am going to treat the next man who shows up in my life like the scumbag that one guy was to me, but from my view now, from a place of pain, every guy is.

But how do we beat this? It's not a matter of not entirely engaging with these 'broken, disappointed and scared for their lives Beings, they just require more gentleness, if you are a man or a woman who meets someone you truly love, you are not going to turn your back or run away from this person because they have been hurt before, because 'I can't deal with something broken'. Don't get me wrong, you cannot save everyone, especially if the situation takes a lot from you, and leaves you drained. One thing you need to understand about pain and negative experiences though, is that you cannot un-experience that, but what you can do instead, is to carry on with the rest of your life with the experience and choose how you allow it to affect your life, will it have a negative effect or are you going to make lemonade out of lemons? And I get that it is easier said than done, but it also isn't entirely impossible. Here is a more visual way to understand it;

Say you went out for lunch with your family to your local fast food restaurant to get burgers, now you get there the vibe is set, you get menus to order from, the waiter or waitress, whomever you would like to imagine being of service to you, takes your order, your mom goes first, ordering a double cheeseburger, one of your cousins orders a classic cheeseburger, your aunt orders a chicken fillet burger, your sister orders a bacon and avocado beef burger, while you on the other hand order a "sweet chilli with crisp onions" beef burger, but when the order arrives, because you are sitting next to your sister, your orders somehow get twisted, well swapped is the right word to use for that, but because the conversations are flowing, you don't even notice until your first bite off your burger and that is when you have this strange taste in your mouth, Avocado!!! You hate Avo, you have never had one before, I mean you have, but you've just never enjoyed the taste of it, and the look of an avocado just disgusts you, now, imagine having a taste of one. But can you 'un-taste' it? Of course not, you are just going to have to go on with the rest of the date with the taste of the avocado in your mouth and not allow it to ruin the lunch date, or you can cause a scene complaining about how the waiter is so untrained because they got your order wrong(or swapped your orders), which causes the restaurant to give you a different or rather extra burger, out of their sincere apologetic hearts, but because of that one bad experience at that restaurant, it causes some envy against waiters and waitresses that builds up in you.

The theory right there is simple, negative experiences are always going to be there, but it is all up to us to choose how to respond to them, we obviously cannot return to the 'we' we once were before those experiences, but we can dictate the "who" we will become in the future even after having had some terrible experiences. Will we allow those experiences to make us bitter and take away our optimism about life, or will we be more cautious, create boundaries and still choose to experience the good side of life without feeling like the world is out there to get us?

CHAPTER 5- MY PARENTS ARE STRICT

Strict parents, caring and compassionate individuals, they are. All they want is to protect their young ones from a world filled with a truth contaminated with pure evil, selfishness, corruption, greed, and a thirst for power. But they are often mistaken for being toxic, however, I understand where they are coming from.

Strict parents, depending on their level of strictness, may come off as parents who are too overprotective and don't want their kids to live their best lives. But that's not always the case. The way we perceive their behaviour or strictness is different from how they view it. For them, being strict means, you'll be safe here, I will protect you and no one will be able to cause harm to you in any way. But what it feels like to the child is "fear being instilled in me to hinder me from making mistakes and taking the lessons that come with those mistakes". Which is sad, but true; strict parents are aware of the reality of this world, more than any of us are, some have had a share of their own medicine in the pain & deceit that this world possesses, and so for them, warning their kids about that and not allowing them out or to do any of the things that they believe will leave their kids in ruins, is a way of them protecting their young ones from what they've been through, or from what they have observed others go through. I mean, I know for a fact that I never want my seed to one day experience or go through the same pain that I have been through or seen others go through, the rape, the emotional abuse, the narcissism, and maybe even death at a young age due to negligence, and that is the same with strict parents.

But of course, we need to learn to distinguish between strict parents and narcissistic parents; strict parents do not necessarily have a personal vendetta or agenda against their own kids, they just want what's best for them, by ensuring that their safety is their top priority, but how do they go about this "safety precaution"? Instead of making their kids aware of the harsh reality of this world and teaching them how to respond to it, how to protect themselves were they to encounter any harshness from life or the world, they instil fear, don't get me wrong, they do make their kids aware of the darkness of the world, but instead of preparing them for "war", they ensure that their kids do not participate in the war at all. For them, not allowing their kids to go out late at night to parties because they are afraid their kids will get intoxicated and might end up getting sexually assaulted or worse, getting involved in a car accident and dying, is a way of protecting their kids. But that's not how life works.

The Creator has given each of us free will, and in as much as parents are guardians of their kids on behalf of the Creator, they cannot decide and make choices for their kids for the rest of their lives. Parents as guardians are there to teach and guide, and instilling fear is not the best way to go about it. There's only much that parents can do for their kids before they too become adults, start a family of their own and have their own kids to guard. Being a guardian means that you teach, yes, you expose the harshness of life & the world to your kids, you make them aware of what is out there, but you also teach them response, that "how do I handle this if or when it happens to me", instead of building up walls that prevent your kids the freedom of exploration. After all, life is all about living, and living about freedom. So, how can one feel free if they aren't allowed the opportunity to make their own choices, without feeling like they are going to choke to their death if they are wrong, or make a mistake?

Freedom does not necessarily mean leaving your kids to roam around the world like headless chickens, no! Freedom is making your kids aware of the two paths in life, one that feels easy and fun, and short to get to your destination, and the other that is longer, challenging, still could be fun if you looked at it from a different perspective, has a few people on it and isn't marketed a lot by the world, or is advertised a lot, (but has been given a distorted image by falsies, and has now led to people doubting its existence, and disallowing them to choose which path they'll take), but without pressurizing them and/or trying to convince them that they will end up in a blazing fire for the rest of their eternity if they don't choose the path that you want them to, rather allowing them to figure out which path exactly they need to choose, by themselves, with the guidance from you as a parent, of course, and not necessarily forcing them, but by taking baby steps with them, being patient with them when they make mistakes, and helping them learn from those mistakes.

Because the truth is; "everything, good or bad, happens because the Creator allows it to", so in as much as parents may not want certain things to happen to their kids, hence, they become overly strict or protective, these things will happen one way or another, if the Creator wills for it to be a part of their story. And I say "one way or another" in the sense that it won't just happen when your kids are out late, getting intoxicated, or wearing revealing items of clothing. It might just happen in the four corners of your own home. The reality of tragedy is that like death, it has no specifications and no slight hint or clue of when, or how, or to whom it will happen. It might just happen in a bathroom at a restaurant where you feel that your kid might be safe, but a druggie who has his life issues and personal agendas might just eye your little girl and end up hurting them. To make things even worse, your husband, the father of your baby could, and might just turn out to be the thief who steals your baby's innocence or your very own dignity.

So, to strict parents, I would say; caging and sheltering your kids all in the name of "I am trying to protect you from the harsh reality of this world" isn't going to protect them, instead, it will leave them defenceless in a time when they'll be faced with tragedy, they will not be prepared enough to know what to do, how to respond and whom to call on. Instead, they will dig a little hole for themselves to bury themselves in, or put up a cage for themselves, like you always have, and hide away, instead of standing up for themselves, they will stand down because no one will have ever taught them how to defend themselves, all they know is how to be afraid, to disengage, because they will be unprepared for the war ahead.

On the other hand, narcissistic parents are just a bowl of some good old vanilla ice cream topped up with a whole lot of toxicity. These are individuals who let out their frustrations, insecurities, and failures onto other people, well, in this case, their kids. These individuals have a lot of shadow work to do, they are individuals who haven't really healed from past abuse or childhood trauma, so, they have found defence mechanisms and coping mechanisms to assist in dealing with their issues, one of those being "making other individuals feel less than they actually are because it strokes their egos and helps in hiding their own insecurities". Narcissistic parents reflect how they feel about themselves onto their children. And it is something like this,

"you are a failure, not because you actually are, every individual gets it wrong the first time before they get it right, but because that is how I've always felt about myself, or that is what I grew up hearing all the time, and it has been embedded so deep inside of me that I cannot unseen myself as that, appreciating who you are as an individual regardless of how hard you try to make me proud is challenging for me, as I'm so used to having the negatives highlighted so much so that I miss the beauty of the effort that comes with trying, and so I push you to work so hard, not from a place of love, but from a place of insecurity which is why it sounds as though I don't really love you or care about you but I just don't know how to, I have basically been operating from a place of insecurity and egotism being depicted as self-confidence and self-awareness from a very young age, which has helped shield my heart from the negativity and hurt I've experienced in my past, but in actual fact, I'm just struggling, struggling to see my own self as worthy of love, which leads to my inability to give you any. And I guess the famous quote "you can't pour out of an empty cup" plays a huge role in my case, because all I'm filled with is bitterness, which all presents itself as toxic behaviours, but as I've already mentioned before, I just need help, I probably don't know where to start, I don't know how to ask for help or to accept it, because I try to act like there's absolutely nothing messed up or wrong with me, just to protect myself. I've been doing that for a while now, and it's become a norm for me, denying my own issues and shifting the spotlight onto someone else's issues, but deep inside I know I've been struggling, so much that if I don't begin with the internal work necessary, I will end up hurting and pushing away everyone close to me who truly and genuinely cares about me, you included".

Narcissistic parents are toxic parents. These are the kind of people who inflict fear onto their kids, they use fear as a way to control their kids, they are the kind of people who inflict pain onto their kids and aren't even ashamed of doing so. Narcissistic parents are very negligent parents who aren't necessarily ready to raise another human being because having a child means that you are sure, well not a hundred percent sure but definitely not thirty percent, that you are ready to, and are in a good state; be it mentally, financially, physically, and emotionally; to raise a decent human being(although kids these days are born out of one-night stands, unplanned pregnancies etc.). Narcissistic parents tend to be bullies, not only to their kids but to other people around them, and what Bullying really is, is that it is a form of emotional abuse, it is seeking or obtaining gratification at the expense of someone else's emotions or recognition. Bullying is intentional, and just like every other action, bullying is a conscious decision one makes. It is a shameful act towards the victim, a violation of their peace and happiness, therefore, because bullying is emotional abuse, and emotions have to do with one's mentality, bullying can lead to emotional turmoil which, as a result, can cause an even more psychological disorder such as depression, and or anxiety, which is associated with low self-esteem to the victim. Before I move further from the topic of bullying and its effects on the victim, and back to the topic of parenting, I would like to divert a little and focus on the perpetrator of such an act. If you look closely at the issue of bullying, you will realize that a lot of times bullies are lost or broken souls who have untreated wounds, and the longer the wound goes untreated, the further the spread of the infection, not only to the patient suffering from the wound but to external parties as well, hence, bullies tend to lash out at their victims. Bullies have their own internal turmoil deep inside that they tend to conceal or mask with either sarcasm or even physical violence. Internal turmoil could vary from lack to envy, so, not having something that their victim has, does not have to be materialistic, it could even be a child without a healthy relationship with their parents or who comes from a background that isn't well off, envying another child who seems to have it all going well for them in their life, but one thing to note from that is that bullies become envious of their victims, and being envious means that they will try by all means to communicate their anger, insecurity, and pain through the abuse on their victim. As already mentioned previously, oftentimes, bullies tend to find that the best way to deal with their frustrations is by way of "concealing" them, but the more they do that, the more built-up emotions they have, hence, when they engage in relationships, they have this toxic energy that they exude as a result of the negative emotions and energies they have stored inside them, which is why it is so important to release any energy that does not serve one's higher self, through various forms of healing like crying, meditation, screaming from the top of one's lungs, punching something(not another person of course), exercising, engaging in anything artsy, listening to music and singing till your oesophagus hurts, laughing until you can no longer feel your teeth in your mouth, seeking help from professionals etc.

I want to touch a bit on copying mechanisms, as bullying is also a form of that. But first, what are coping mechanisms? Coping mechanisms are tools used to deal with a situation that has caused one to be in a negative state of mind. What are some of the examples of coping mechanisms, you ask? Well, there are two types of coping mechanisms, one being healthy coping mechanisms, and the other being unhealthy. Healthy coping mechanisms are those that contribute to the upliftment and positive wellbeing of oneself, and unhealthy coping mechanisms are short-term fulfilling pleasures that can be addictive but do not contribute positively to one's wellbeing. So, what are the types of Healthy and Unhealthy coping mechanisms? Healthy coping mechanisms include confronting one's pain and emotions and not shying away from them, they involve things like therapy, and some of the activities I have just mentioned above, relating to the release of negative energy, whereas, on the other hand, unhealthy coping mechanisms involve the use of substances such as drugs, alcohol, and smoking thereof, which ultimately leads to the abuse of such substances, but don't get me wrong, prescribed medication(drugs) can be a healthy coping mechanism only, and only if it is not overused or underused, and by that I mean when one does not use more than prescribed or does not go the extra mile of trying to obtain such medication like 'anti-depressants', without a doctor's recommendation or approval, if so, then it becomes unhealthy. But bullying is also a coping mechanism, and it is a type of unhealthy coping mechanism. Bullies, as we have concluded in the previous section, have their own demons they are fighting within, some of these people are people who lost their parents at an early stage of their childhood and are finding it difficult to navigate through life thus they take out their frustrations onto other individuals, some are people who have a void that needs to be filled, for example; they themselves, do not feel as though they are enough, and that is; not beautiful enough, smart enough, or even cool enough, hence, they try to bring others down to their level by making comments that are insulting and diminishing, just because that is a reflection of how they feel inside about themselves, and it makes them feel better to see others suffer like they are, and other times, bullies are attention-seeking individuals(and that is maybe because they do not receive the attention from those they wish to), who will do or say anything just to impress people even if it is on the expense of someone else's emotions, feelings, well-being, let alone life.

Moving on from the topic of bullying and back to the topic of parenting, having a child shouldn't be a prize or a cause for celebration of "I have made it in life, I am not infertile, I am a man,

I am a woman, I am able to conceive and birth life", but it also shouldn't be something that scares or frightens one. Of course, having a baby is something beautiful and worth celebrating, but having a child is a lot of work, raising another human being requires a certain level of maturity. One thing to note is that having a child isn't just about affordability, because you can have all the money in the world and still raise an unhappy, unhealthy child. Having a child should be considered a blessing, but one needs to be ready for the emotional maturity that comes with raising a child. Having a child is a gift from the Creator of life, for you to give life, to birth someone, however, a child comes with great responsibility, and so many times kids are born into families that aren't prepared enough to give or offer them the stability they require. Of course, financial stability is a major factor to consider when you want to have kids but that shouldn't be the only thing you consider.

Kids are like sponges, they absorb energies. Kids, infants to be specific, take on the different aspects from their parent's personalities, I mean, of course, everyone is born different, with their own personalities, likes, and dislikes, but these aren't so evident in the beginning stages of one's life cycle. When a child is born, there are so many things to learn, from crawling to teething, to walking, and talking, these are things that, although natural, kids absorb from the people around them, which, they themselves, imitate. The upbringing of a child influences the man and woman he or she will turn out to be, and yes, we all have free will and choices to make, but your background has a big influence on how you behave, view the world, and interact with those around you.

As a parent, your values, your ethics or morals, your standards, and your beliefs play a huge role in the upbringing of your child. Your values are your convictions with regards to what is good, whereas your ethics, also referred to as morals are; accepted, responsible behaviours, which are not only good for yourself, but for others too. Ethics are the thin line that exists between what is considered good and what is considered bad. Your standards on the other hand are a level of attainment that you as an individual consider as acceptable. All these components are very much inherent to the child from the parent. This then makes sense as to why you, as an individual need to ensure that you are putting in the work into yourself to ensure that you will be a better human not only to yourself but to your kids and the world around you.

A lot of broken adults are kids who either grew up in terrible backgrounds, or who have had terrible childhood experiences, which is something that you have probably come across from some quote or article off the internet, but which is also very much true. As mentioned before, your experiences as a child will shape the kind of individual you will become as an adult, unless you put in the work as an adult to heal from your negative past experiences, in order to live and experience life from a more holistic place. However, if you do not put in the work to become whole, you will suffer a great deal of your childhood trauma, hurt, and insecurities even throughout your adulthood.

CHAPTER 6- WELCOME TO THE RAPE CAPITAL

The fact that a young lady should be warned against going out late, wearing a short skirt or shorts that leave a quarter of her bum hanging out all in the name of "young girls are being raped/abducted to be used for human trafficking" should make men feel disgusted, disgusted over the fact that they have created and continue to create a world infused with fear, but it should most importantly teach men, teach them self-discipline, teach them love, self-confidence, and strengthen them, because being violent against a woman by a man does not in any way display strength, but rather weakness. Because a strong man would be able to control his urges to rape a woman, let alone an infant. A strong man would know that the feminine energy is not weak but strong and laying his hand on someone who possesses that quality means that he is weak because strength should never be drawn from making another Being feel inferior.

And I think that's where the issue is, the reality is that the world is a harsh place to live in. In South Africa for example, gender based violence is commonly initiated by people from foreign countries, and although these foreigners are very much engaging in such tedious activities to harm our young girls, so are our own people(not to say we are not one with these foreigners, but just for distinguishing purposes). Our brothers and fathers are the rapists, thieves, and butchers, and not to say that women are not involved in some of these operations, but most of the victims are women and the perpetrators, men. Now, after having done some introspection, I do realize that my mother was trying to protect my sister and I, from the very same people who would one day turn out to be the perpetrators of our pain. When my mother would refuse us the freedom of dressing up in whatever kind of way we wished to, around the house, especially when the items of clothing were too revealing, she was doing it out of the fear that whatever spirit that was and still is possessing the male specie, would one day possess our father or one of our brothers and the worst would happen. But what happened to self-control? - I wonder! That "I'm tempted, I'm fully aware of that, I can feel that I am about to lose control over my emotions and feelings, and I might end up doing something tedious or uncalled for, but I'm going to choose to look away or walk away because I know that it is wrong, and I am aware of the repercussions that would follow this feeling or thought that I am about to act on." What ever happened to that?

Being a young lady in a country considered the rape capital i.e., South Africa, for me, always meant that I would one day be a statistic of the number of women who have been raped. I always had to be a little more cautious than my male peers because I was at the risk of being sexually assaulted. Every time a male figure would approach me, I had to, and still have to keep my guard up and I bet they sense the scare in my eyes, as they begin to enter into my world, questioning what it is they want from me, if it is the beauty of my mind they are interested in, or the curves of my body they desire? Whether they wish to swim in the pool of my past and dreams, or whether it is the well of my soul that is in between my thighs they long to drown in?

Gender-based violence isn't a movement that started a few seconds ago, this has been an ongoing issue that women and men have been faced with since the early centuries and is now getting louder because more and more individuals are becoming open about their experiences.

Rape, as defined by the South African Police Services(SAPS) is "The penetration, no matter how slight, of the vagina or anus with any body part or object, or oral penetration by a sex organ of another person, without the consent of the victim, it is the intentional, unlawful sexual intercourse with a woman without her consent.

Sexual intercourse includes the penetration of the labia majora (outer lips of the vulva) and not just the labia minora".

[And yes, maybe the definition shouldn't be so gender specific.]

The different types of rape that exist, but are not limited to, as read on Wikipedia, are;

Date Rape, which consists of two forms of Rape, namely; an acquaintance rape, occurring between two individuals who, somewhat know each other, such as lovers i.e. boyfriend and girlfriend, people who are in the beginning stages of a relationship (still flirting or getting to know one another but haven't concluded a solid agreement of being in a relationship), between friends or even just acquaintances(strangers who are somewhat familiar with one another), so that can be your neighbour, a random boy/girl, or a man/woman you met and exchanged contacts with, but aren't necessarily friends with, your co-worker or colleague, or your employer, a classmate or schoolmate, a family member, your teacher from school, or lecturer from University/College etc., and the other form of date rape being DFSA, which is short for drug-facilitated sexual assault, which occurs on the intention of the perpetrator to incapacitate the victim with any drug that incapacitates another person, leaving them susceptible to any form of sexual assault, rape included.

Gang Rape is the rape of a single victim by multiple persons or by a group of people.
This type of rape is said to most likely occur late at night when there is alcohol and drug intoxication involved, with less resistance from the victim due to probably intoxication and/or fear.

Spousal Rape, which is also known as marital rape, husband rape, wife rape, partner rape, or IPSA, which stands for 'intimate partner sexual assault', is a form of violence in a domestic setting and is abusive sexual behaviour. This kind of rape can be hard to come into terms with or even realize because "we are married, I am supposed to give into any sexual act that my partner may require from me at any point in time that my partner requires me to do so", but that isn't true, married or not, you shouldn't be forced into any sexual act if you do not want.

Child Rape is a form of sexual abuse against the child. This rape can happen between an older child and a younger child, between a parent/guardian/close relative and a child, a stranger, a teacher, someone in a religious authority position, etc. If the rape is by a relative, it is considered incest, which refers to any form of human sexual behaviour between close relatives, relationship determined by the level of blood relations and relations in law, including relations through adoption or clans. This kind of rape is like statutory rape but does not have the age restriction like statutory rape does.

Statutory Rape is a form of rape perpetrated on a child who cannot give consent. A child in this case is a minor, someone who is under the age of 18 in South Africa and most probably other African countries, but 16 in other non- African countries.

Prison Rape is commonly a same sex/gender type of rape, mostly between inmates, as a result of prisoners being grouped by gender or sex in jail cells, but even though that is the case, that does not always mean that the perpetrator is interested in the same gender as themselves, but could stem from what could be so evident such as a result of a lack of sexual activity for a very long time from being locked up in jail for a while.

Serial Rape is a repetitive form of rape by one unknown perpetrator to various victims who are targeted by the rapist. In most cases, the rapist or perpetrator of such an act follows a plan or pattern which can easily be predicted, for instance, the rapist may be into young kids or may target older women who stay alone at home, it all depends on the rapist's preferences. However, it is common that these kinds of individuals are smart in their approach because they do not want to be caught or discovered by law enforcement, they may strategically remove any evidence from the scene that may assist the police in finding them.

Revenge Rape, also known as payback rape or punishment rape, is a form of rape between tribes or cultures and is usually perpetrated on a female, that is meant to bring some form of shame on the male in her tribe for the humiliation they may have caused the tribe perpetrating the rape by performing some acts against that other tribe. It is quite similar to **War Rape**, as the rape is meant to bring about humiliation to the enemy of the perpetrator. **War Rape** is a form of rape that is perpetrated during armed conflicts or war and may include forced prostitution or sexual slavery on the hostages.

Deceptive Rape is a rape that occurs through false pretences of power by the perpetrator to gain the agreement of the victim. The perpetrator may threaten to harm the victim by pretending to hold somewhat a high position which would allow him to follow through with the threat all for the sake of engaging in some form of sexual activity with the victim.

Corrective Rape, which, all thanks to South African law exists, is a form of rape against homosexual individuals to punish them for switching gender roles, and/or to make them 'straight'.

Custodial Rape is rape perpetrated by your police officers, jail employees, nurses, doctors, caregivers of orphans in an orphanage, or any other member of the staff who has been placed in a custodial position by the state.

Rape is a cruel act against humanity. I, like many individuals used to think that rape was violent, but rape isn't always forceful, rape does not always entail weapons, or holding someone down against their will, it's not always going to look like that, rape can be coercion, rape can be sweet, sweet manipulation.

Rape does not have a category, it can and may happen to just anyone, and anywhere. Rape is not an "oh she's out late at night getting intoxicated so that's my type", or "she's wearing a short skirt, or she has her chest out so she's asking for it", rape does not have a type. It is a weakness on the perpetrator's part. Oftentimes, people use rape as a way to exert power over another individual because they lack empathy, but rape is not a sense or measure of power, rape is a cry for help, because "This thing has got a hold on me, like a possessive demon, and I cannot control myself when the urge comes up, so I end up forcing myself onto innocent people, I end up bruising them and I just- I just lack the self-control".

Rape is; "I thought I found the perfect opportunity where vulnerability exists, and thought no one would find out, and I thought I would get away with it, so I did it, but it went around and bit me right in the ass".

Having said so much about such a violent act, I can conclude by saying that I cannot wait for a world that strives to be "RARE" i.e., Rape, Abuse, & Richism-Eradicated.

As a result of this Rape Culture trend, the kids of our generation hardly ever get to fully experience their innocence, because they get robbed of it when they involuntarily get exposed to sexual, physical, and emotional violence at an early stage of their childhood. It has become extremely hard for parents or guardians to not stress or worry about the safety of their child(ren) when they get exposed to the world and the different strangers roaming around, or when they (the parents) place them in the care of someone other than themselves, because of the fear that their child(ren) might have some of their rights violated. The youth, the middle-aged, and the old-aged find their lives endangered. Trust is something that has been broken over the years, and not to say that it will never again come easy, but it's going to take a while to be earned again. On top of that, being approached by a random stranger just brings a tingling sensation down one's spine, which is the fear of the unknown- fear of what might happen if not in the next couple of seconds or minutes of one's engagement with the stranger, so, a lot of us would rather ignore those strangers who come up to us, trying to strike up a conversation because we are too afraid and are trying to prevent anything bad from happening to us. But is it only the strangers we are afraid of? As I've mentioned before, trust has been broken over the last couple of years, and I would like to make clear the fact that it isn't the trust between you as an individual and a random stranger. It's crystal clear how the world as we see it has been tarnished with such evil and pain, and as a result, it has become hard to look at with Rose coloured glasses.

I used to think, growing up, that Rape would be initiated by a stranger, uneducated, homeless, and with no morals or standards whatsoever, not that I was ignorant, but because I had so much faith in the men close to me, I did not want to believe that they would engage in such a horrendous act, a little optimistic, maybe? But now? I am not really scared of the man on the corner street begging for food or money, who looks like they haven't had a shower in decades, and haven't had a meal for who knows how long? I'm not! However, I'm scared of the "high status" guy. He's too nice, and he lures you into trusting him, making you believe that he has your best interest at heart, he traps you into believing that he's "the good guy", that he is absolutely not capable of those horrible things that are said to be done to women and children by men, and you know what happens? Because of this image that he's painted of himself, you become so trusting, you fall right into his trap! How naive of you that you want to believe so bad that there's a little good in this dark-filled world. But by the time you realize the kind of person he really is, it's too late, because you have fallen into that hell hole, he has dug up for you, so deep, and so dark that it feels surreal, like a nightmare. And so, just like in a nightmare you have nowhere to escape to, you're trapped, trapped in his web of lies. And now all he does to you is take, what is rightfully yours! Without your consent he continues to take, bruising your poor soul, does he care if you're okay!? Not really, because all he ever cared about was his desires and needs - self-satisfaction and selfishness, that is! He invades sacred parts of your soul, uninvitedly so, as he explores the waves of your ocean. This man possessively lays hold of your entirety. The man you should be afraid of is the one who's had a shower a couple of hours ago, who's had a full-on breakfast meal, the one with a nice titled job, the one who is respected by family members and the community, the one whom people look up to but has sicko motives and tricks under his sleeves, he's the one that's broken but doesn't realize it, so he continues to break others to become just like him. And I don't mean to paint a bad name for the men who possess those qualities because the truth is that you can never know who the wolf will be, some people will walk into your life, appearing to be exactly like the man I have just described, but they'll be different, because they will have pure, genuine intentions with you, but how will you know? You won't, so I guess you are going to have to trust your instincts, use your intuition, you will feel it, you will just know it because your intuition levels will be heightened up, but also, you're going to have to seek discernment from God, to open your spiritual eyes to see who truly is being genuine and who isn't. You are probably wondering, are your views on how and why rape occurs, a little different because it hits home now? Of course! See, we often get mad and frustrated over individuals who give nonchalant responses when rape occurs to someone we know, a stranger, or even to us, because how dare they act as if it isn't such a big deal? But in every situation in life, when you're viewing things from a rear view or a side mirror when something isn't as personal to you, it can be hard to relate to and sympathize with someone who is going through that, but just because something isn't personal to you, it doesn't mean that you shouldn't show compassion towards another individual who might be going through it, whether you know both sides to a story or not. This message not only applies to family and friends, but to the individuals who form part of the justice system as well.

A lot of women and men who have had their rights violated, be it physically or sexually, often make comments about the police services, and the criminal justice system being useless, because oftentimes when you are a man and you make your way to the station to report that you have been physically abused/assaulted by a woman, the officers make fun of you, because what kind of man gets overpowered by a woman? That must mean that you aren't man enough, to have a woman sexually assault you, how is that even possible? When a woman makes her way to the station to report how her boyfriend physically abuses her, they make jokes like "oh well, these two always play like this, don't take them seriously", or even though they take your statement, they give you weird looks and make funny remarks that make you think they do not believe what you are saying, but are just entertaining you to follow protocol because that's their job.

This is why you find people choosing to not report any form of violation against themselves because they are afraid of being made fun of, scared of being so vulnerable, and putting their faith in a system, to save and protect them. But the issue with the justice system is that it is just that – a system, it isn't a saviour, it is a system that has been put in a place to try and bring about justice to people who have been offended, by looking at all the different available information that can be used as evidence and after having done that, making an informed decision which will be fair, and just to both parties involved, that being the offender and the offended.

Even so, the problem remains that "it is run by humans who are just like you and me, humans who have emotions and external factors that influence their judgement as they make these "just and fair" decisions". Sometimes they have to put their feelings and emotions aside and just be practical, to really try and solve a case, and that can sometimes bring anger and bitterness to an individual who does not receive a perceived outcome, especially when they know deep inside that they were truthful about the offense perpetrated against them, but because the evidence they submitted was not substantial enough to prove the offender as guilty, or was not as believable because, perhaps the incident happened a while ago but the justice system was too preoccupied with other important work piled up for them to complete and could only solve the case after a few years following the incident, and as a result, the offended could not remember every detail regarding the assault as they had been trying to forget, find closure on their own, heal and move on with their life, which leads to them jinxing things up for themselves by changing up information and just making things seem to not add up when asked questions relating to the assault.

Which I find so absurd, why does it have to take so long to receive justice from our criminal justice system? If my story does not receive any media coverage, then best believe that I will not be first priority. Why do I have to wait years for me to finally get my voice to be heard and see my perpetrator reap the consequences of his actions? But then again, I realize that most times as victims of crime, we're only looking for closure, expecting the criminal justice system to defend you as you were defenceless during an act of crime against you is totally understandable, but to try and seek closure, to say that I will only heal and be at peace once my perpetrator has been arrested? That is setting yourself up for a lot of disappointment. I mean, for sure, an offender of crime should be removed from the community, as they pose as a danger to society, and locking them away will somewhat make you feel safe, safe in the sense that you know that they will never be able to hurt you again, at least not when they are locked up in jail, and hopefully that they will never get the chance to hurt any other person, ever.

But here's the thing with closure, closure isn't something you get, it is something that you create for yourself. A lot of people find it difficult to move past terrible experiences because "well, I need closure". But you are never going to receive that, because in order for you to heal and move past something, something that has been done to you, you are going to have to accept that it has happened, you then need to realize that regardless of what has happened to you, or what has been done to you, life still goes on, therefore, you need to learn how to adapt and adjust with the pain inside of you and carry on with life, but also learning how to let go or to release that pain, and that is what we call healing.

CHAPTER 7- MY HISTORY OF DATING & SEXUALITY

Dating, well, on earth, is part of every adolescent's journey in their lifetime, and it was no different for me. My love life started in my first year of high school. I had always been the kind of girl who was too scared of boys, not that I didn't see them as alluring or attractive in any way, but just because my parents- my mom and aunts to be specific, always lectured me about the 7B's. Now, if you aren't aware of what the 7B's are, allow me to elaborate; the 7B's was and hopefully still isn't a phrase a mother would use on their daughter, so as to avoid having to hold the whole conversation on why they feel that their daughter should not be having a "boyfriend", and I say it in quotation because the honest truth is as the human race, we have attached to this word a negative connotation, which means that the opposite genders cannot befriend one another because all they will ever want to do together is to get sexual and physical, and thus discouraging the existence of many platonic relationships between the male and female. The 7B's basically mean "Books Before Boys Because Boys Bring Babies". Most women who were born before the 21st century, unlike modern parents who are rather more open-minded, find it challenging to have such open conversations with their daughters, conversations about why their daughters shouldn't be fooling around with boys because "boy meets girl, girl meets boy, boy says I love you and so does she, boy tells girl to come over to the house because parents aren't home, and girl agrees to meet up, when girl meets boy at house, the following happens; boy and girl sitting in a tree K-I-S-S-I-N-G, first comes baby in the baby carriage, sucking his thumb and wetting his pants, never comes love, and never comes marriage, oh what a waste on young love", and the reason for this challenge most parents face, of being open and transparent with their daughters about this, is because they themselves have never found themselves being sat down by their own parents to discuss such matters, because in the past; everyone would just let nature take its course.

However, before I came to this realization that I am about to share with you, of course, I used to blame my parents for being closed-minded, as if it were something that they did on purpose, and that they were just too stubborn to not want to change the way things were in the past, but once I began to recognize that everyone is assigned their own different responsibility and role in life, and that only you can fulfil what you have been appointed for, that's when I realized that, as much as my parents did not want to change, and failed to switch things up, it remains my responsibility to change that narrative. It is really up to me to decide on whether I will one day choose to also not hold the conversation of dating and sexing at a young age with my daughter or son, just like my parents chose to not have that conversation with me, or if I will engage in such conversations with my children because they are important, and it is my responsibility to teach and guide my children and prepare them for the world ahead.

What I find quite interesting though is that there isn't a saying or talk that is directed specifically to boys, advising them on staying away from girls. Girls are the only ones who have to "guard their hearts", but ever thought of it like this; girls wouldn't have to guard their hearts if boys were also being taught these things, what things, you ask? Dating, what dating entails. Love, how to give and receive love(both romantic, platonic and a love towards self). Marriage, what it means, how to know when you are ready and have finally found that one individual to commit to. Sex, the beauty, and dangers of sex, all these things. But don't worry kids, you've got aunty Rilonde to bail you out on this one, so, here's a little relationship series for you guys; but before I dive right into it, I just want to say, I know what you've been told, that there isn't a recipe or formula to relationships or dating, that you just have to wing it because we are all different and what we need and want in our particular relationships may differ from what other people want or need in theirs, but I'm here NOT to tell you otherwise, because that is very much true, but there are a few things that are important in all relationships, we can perhaps call these the most basic, yet essential elements that make a relationship what it is. This is a 7(seven) part series, meaning it has subtopics to it, the first being Detach, followed by Date Yourself, Intentions, Expectations, Boundaries, then Communication is key, and lastly A Single Entity. These are all mini parts in the series, basically breaking down what to expect in relationships; the lovers' kind, that is. I don't really touch a lot on sex in this series because I have a chapter dedicated to you, focusing only on sex, and that is because it is that sacred, so here goes;

PT.1 DETACH

Now, this is especially for my people who were previously in a relationship.

Before you get into your next relationship, you need to let go of all your baggage from your previous/past commitments. Leave all of your bad habits and attachments behind. And I am not saying that you need to become this completely different, new person, sort of forgetting all that you were before the ending of your previous relationship, but for me personally, I find that taking time off before entering into a next relationship having just left another, is very necessary, not because I'm still holding onto that past relationship and I cannot move on from it, but because I'm healing, unlearning some of the bad traits that I may have unknowingly taken on from that connection, literally detaching myself from that connection.

A lot of times we want to get away from something so much, that we're willing to get onto the next bus as soon as we can, just so the past cannot catch up with us. And I have heard this quite a lot of times, that taking a gap or break in between your previous relationship and your next is only necessary because "you need to find yourself again" and thus most people find it to be unnecessary, as "they had never lost themselves" in a previous connection, but being realistic, you cannot just walk out of a relationship you were once emotionally invested in and be done, like D, O, N, E, never! There's a part of you that's going to go on nostalgic mode, reminiscing on the good and not so good memories you once shared with your ex-partner, or that one altercation you both got into, which caused your first break-up and so you thought that was the end of you guys, but things ended up working out between you two. Therefore, getting into a new relationship having not released yourself, or detached completely from that previous relationship, will only be for rebound purposes.

However, If you do this, i.e. take time out for yourself before entering into a newer connection, you give yourself the chance and opportunity to re-evaluate, you re-evaluate what you're actually looking for in a relationship, you create boundaries for yourself, what you will and what you will not tolerate from a partner in a relationship, the boundaries that you need to set in place so that you and your partner can have a healthy relationship, and lastly, you heal, heal from past wounds that the previous relationship may have inflicted onto you just so you don't transmit your insecurities and fears from old wounds onto your next relationship, although that can be very difficult when you have loved fully, and wholly, and have had that love taken for granted, have had someone ruin your perfect little idea of what love is or can be, through betrayal and disappointment, but the good news is that there is always room to try again.

If, however, you were not in a previous relationship, then you need to position your mind in the right direction. And that is; because you were previously never attached or tied to someone else, you had all the desired freedom in your life, to yourself, you did not have to check up on anyone, you may have even been reckless in your decisions, but if you meet a new love interest and you realize the potential that is in front of you, to build a relationship with, then you are going to have to leave most of your old habits behind. Because things are now going to have to be a little different. You can't walk into something new with the same mindset you held in the past. But also, we are all toxic in some way, and toxic doesn't have to be anything bad like "narcissism, or physical/emotional abuse", but sometimes the values and views that you may hold may differ from someone else's and when that individual's soul does not resonate with it, they may view you as "toxic" to their energy, and we cannot make everyone happy of course, but sometimes, especially in relationships, you need to be open to the idea that your partner's views, let alone upbringing, may differ from yours and be receptive to change.

Detach from old habits, relations, and thinking patterns, to fully function as your truest form of self in the new!

Pt.2 Date yourself

I know this sounds very cliché, but it is extremely important.

It is important that before you enter into a commitment with somebody, you see yourself as datable, because if you do not have that particular view of yourself, then how do you expect somebody else to find you "datable" or likable? It is like not seeing your own potential and expecting someone else to somehow dig it up until they find it. If you don't value yourself or see yourself as "worthy" of receiving love and giving it in return, then there's no way you are going to value the love you will receive from your partner. So, what does it mean to 'date yourself'?

It is so simple, it is taking yourself out, out on dates, breakfast dates, lunch dates, dinner dates, just doing random stuff of appreciation for yourself. Spoil yourself with gifts now and again, it does not have to be big. Give yourself the love, you feel and know you deserve, even before you enter into a connection with somebody else. You need to ensure that you are "whole" before you tip toe into someone else's life. And what do I mean by "Whole"? Being whole does not necessarily mean that you have to have everything in check or in place before establishing a relationship with someone, it doesn't mean that you must have achieved all your dreams, goals, and life's purpose, because what would be the point of a life partner then, if you are not going to continuously grow, evolve and enjoy life's bliss together? But what I mean by the term "whole" is that you are complete on your own, you have done some self-work and you realize that only you can make yourself happy, you don't need any person to come and fulfil your desires because you are very much capable of that, but you want them to. It means that you realize your worth and that you seek no external validation to fill a void inside you, being whole just means that you realize that a relationship is a want and not necessarily a need, because whether you're in one or not, you are still able to wander around this world fulfilling your purpose on your own, and so when you come together with another person in unity, you have your own purpose and so do they, and you basically align your purposes together into one greater purpose.

Before you are someone else's, remember that you are your own, thus you need to treat yourself the way that you want to be treated.

Pt.3 Intentions

Intention is being straightforward about what you require from another individual. Intention is letting go of the vagueness and expressing what it is you are drawn to in the other person.

When you tip toe into someone's life, you must at least be clear about your agenda or motives about that person. And I don't say this coming from a negative state like we are all out to use people, but in all honesty, we do want to gain something from the connections we make with other individuals. For instance, when you are seeking to be close with someone because you want a friendship from them, it's not just limited to that because these days friendship is such a vast relationship which embodies a variety of needs in one. Some friendships are just for companionship, for example, "we are just friends who go out to Groove together", whereas others consist of emotional Intimacy, in the sense that one can share and have deep conversations and not just surface-level conversations in the friendship. Whereas other friendships aren't necessarily friendships but really just "acquaintanceships", like those people you know but aren't necessarily close with, those "when I see you on the street, I'll greet you and whatever, but I'd never pick up the phone at 2 in the morning to call you during an emergency kind of relationship", you get?

Any who, intention is necessary especially when it comes to establishing boundaries. Boundaries are super important in relationships, if you want respect to be the foundation of your relationship(s), then set boundaries in place. What boundaries do is to let the other person know how far is too far with you, like if we're just "Groove Mates" then there are certain things about each other's lives we shouldn't be nosy about because it's none of our concern. Intention also just makes the other person aware of where they stand in your life, you know. It reduces the chances of getting mixed signals because the other individual or you, won't have to make assumptions about your place in the other person's life. And so, in the lover's kind of relationship, intention will sort of give the other person a sense of direction on whether you guys are just "smash mates, no strings attached", or "together because we want to one day build a future together".

Make your intentions clear, so as to remove the blindfolds on what really is.

Pt.4 Expectations

You need to clearly communicate what your expectations in a relationship are.

I believe expectations and love languages work hand in hand. **The few most common love languages are as follows**(although I find these to be very boxing);

o   Words of Affirmation,
o   Acts of Service,
o   Receiving Gifts,
o   Quality Time, and
o   Physical Touch.

If you are one who loves spending quality time with your partner, then clearly communicate your expectation for your partner to make time to see you and spend time with you(although this is quite a general requisite in every relationship). If you, however, prefer words of affirmation over physical touch, you need to let your partner know that they shouldn't be all touchy-touchy with you as a way of showing that they "love you". If you like receiving gifts more than giving, then make your partner aware of that, because if they're expecting to receive something all the time then they will be setting themselves up for disappointment.

Expressing your expectations to your partner is vital in your relationship, as it establishes an understanding and agreement as to what the relationship entails. To break that down a little further; If you are only looking for something short-term, then you're clearly not going to expect your partner to be as committed as they would be in a long-term relationship.

Therefore, know what you require in a relationship and communicate those expectations so that you and your partner can reach common ground on how to work around your expectations to build a healthy, fulfilling relationship.

Pt.5 Boundaries

When people say "the relationship you have with others is a true reflection of the kind of relationship you have with yourself", I totally agree with them, and here's why; I'm very compassionate, I know there are things that I struggle with, things that I might not fully be wise on, and instead of judging someone and giving them a side-eye when they struggle with something in a relationship with me (be it platonic or whatever), I'm most likely to be understanding and tolerant because I too often give myself chance, after chance, after chance, without beating myself up, as long as I am willing to learn and change and take the necessary measures to actively work towards that change.

But also, there are times when if someone does not respect me, I am not going to sit around and entertain the disrespect, because with the kind of relationship I have with myself, I am always going to choose myself, I love and respect myself, therefore, if, in the kind of relationship I have with someone else, I realize that they aren't choosing me, and not because they are choosing themselves but because out of utter disrespect they have other options they are entertaining besides me while they are busy leading me on, then I will not hesitate to walk away from that connection, no matter how bad I want it or want to stay. That sounds healthy, right? Right. However, the not so healthy part of it is when one doesn't have healthy boundaries or any boundaries at all within a relationship with themselves; that means that one will most likely end up in toxic situations and stay even when they are pretty much aware of the toxicity, here's an example;

If one struggles with say; 'saying no to themselves or denying themselves certain things for the right reasons of course', like, if you know you like spending money and you can't say no to buying yourself things which are way out of your budget, then you are most likely to struggle with saying no in relationships with other people, your budget is the boundary and you spending more than you had budgeted for is you crossing that boundary. Take it like this, if you're used to giving yourself excuses for certain behaviours and attitudes, you're most likely to make excuses for a partner, family member, or friend.

Let us start light with these examples; you know you don't like being called a certain name by your friend because it makes you feel undervalued or disrespected, and you communicate that to them, by doing so you are "setting a boundary" like, 'this is what I will not tolerate', but even after you have communicated your feelings towards your friend for being called by whatever name, they persist on calling you that, but because of your lack of boundaries, you are likely to give an excuse of "oh well, they are just fooling around they don't really mean to call me that", whereas they, on the other hand, are clearly ignoring your feelings and doing what pleases them instead. Another example would be a sexual boundary in a relationship with your partner; if you know you do not like being touched a certain way, or touched in a particular area and you communicate about that fact to your partner, however, he or she continues to maybe "grab your ass in public", that is them crossing boundaries, and so, if you are used to making boundaries for yourself and not sticking to them, the chances of you having healthy relationships with healthy boundaries with others that aren't crossed are going to be a bit challenging for you.

But let us not act as though influence does not play a huge role in relationships. All of our relationships with individuals somewhat influence the kind of individual we are, be it positively or negatively, and the reason I am touching on the word 'influence' is that your boundaries can be affected by this, sometimes it's not even that you don't have boundaries set in place, it may happen that you do have boundaries but the person(s) you are connecting with may influence you to cross those boundaries or in other terms; "cause you to break the rules".

In essence, boundaries are a steppingstone to creating relationships that are not only favourable to one individual but both parties involved in the relationship.

Pt.6 Communication Is Key

I know you are probably aware of this quotation "communication is key", but I have a feeling that most people always just assume that communication in relationships simply means that we have to check in on one another all day and every day, however, that is not even a major part of communication in connections, because communication is all about knowing how to communicate. And there is so much lack in that regard with so many connections.

Knowing "how to" communicate is so important in the sense that you realize that silence is communication as well.

Silent communication is toxic, and even more heart-breaking when compared to expressing how you truly feel towards the other partner and having your words hurt them. Imagine a situation where you and your partner were getting along pretty well, and then all of a sudden they start ignoring you, and so now the issue comes in when you want to fix things, but you don't know how to because you have no idea on what you might have done to make them upset, you don't even know if they will pay you any attention because they are just acting all unbothered by absolutely anything you do or say, so they might just not take you seriously.

Aggressive communication is also toxic, it is those kinds of conversations that come from nowhere, you will be in the middle of a meal and someone just randomly starts a conversation to a point where it almost gets you choking on your food, because instead of getting their point through to you, they argue, shout, scream and kick just so the other person i.e. you, in this case, can understand where they are coming from, but when in all honesty they do not even have to fight to try and voice out their concerns, issues or any point they may be trying to get through.

Civil communication on the other hand is where you are both mature in how you communicate, you don't hold back on what you want to say and you don't come off as someone who is fighting a war in world war 2, but instead, you sit the other person down, let them know there is something you have been meaning to talk to them about, and lay your heart or concerns on the table. This kind of conversation leaves no room for judgement, you will feel safe to share whatever you have been meaning to open up about to your partner.

Communication isn't just those Good morning, how was your day, and Goodnight texts or calls, yes, of course, those are essential in a relationship because it is always the little things that count and matter. After all, if you truly care about someone you are going to want to know about their well-being, all right? But one thing to note is that;

"Communication might be key but knowing how to communicate is like using your fingerprints to unlock the door because you can never lose that key! It is the secret weapon to unlock someone's heart or mind.

Pt.7 A Single Entity

If you are not aware yet then let me make you aware of this; "Before you say 'I do agree to commit to being with you and you alone for the rest of my eternity' to someone, in front of God and the congregation or your family. Before signing the legal binding documentations before some government official or there by home affairs, you are a single entity, you do not belong to anyone, and no one belongs to you!"

The only reason separations and heartbreaks hurt as much as they do is due to "entitlement". The minute you start telling yourself that you are in a relationship with someone and that means your partner is "yours", then you are in for a shock, because sometimes certain people aren't necessarily meant to stay in your life forever. You can be in a relationship that in your view seems perfect but have an unexpected turn of events happen and end up breaking the two of you apart and if you have that mindset of "this person is mine forever and ever, amen", then it won't be as easy to let go of that person. Don't get me wrong, I am in no way saying to not invest fully in a relationship with someone you are fully drawn to, but what I'm saying rather is that do not ever, I repeat, ever, feel entitled to anyone or anything, your relationship included.

Some people are in your life to help you learn, to mould & shape you before you finally meet that one person you truly desire to spend the rest of your life with- your life partner. And so, there's absolutely nothing wrong with full commitment to a person you are not yet "married" to, but just don't ever make that mistake of thinking you or the other person is bound to stay in that relationship forever because if we are being honest, there isn't any legal binding form/ agreement between you two if you are just dating. And so, knowing that you are a single entity on your own whilst dating, protects both you and the other person from having your hearts shattered when or if the connection comes to an end.

And so, to tell you about my dating history, I'll start by sharing this disclaimer with you "I did not know all this dating advice that I have just offered you, so, please don't judge me".

I started dating this boy in my first year of high school, we were both new to the school, like many other juniors. I had seen him before, well, back in primary school. He used to go to a different school from mine which consisted of both a primary, and high school, and he stayed in a different Kasi from mine, however, we used the same transport between home and school. He was one of those cool kids and honestly, I never thought I stood a chance with him because unlike him, I did not have much of a dating history, and well, he looked like he knew the game and was actually on top of it.

The very first time we locked eyes was during the assembly (the assembly is a gathering of learners and the school staff in the morning before school commences, to give out announcements and to start off the day in prayer), but I did not think that he noticed me, he was standing with friends, chatting, and I just happened to be looking his way. After the assembly, we were walking back to our classes, I was in 8th grade as already mentioned, but we had about 3 classes for the 8th grade, classes A, B, and C. Our school was big, so you can imagine why I must have thought that he hadn't noticed me, because out of the hundred pupils in that school, how do I get noticed? Anyways, my insecurities were just kicking in, we were however not in the same class, I was in class C and he was in class A, and to my surprise, he walked right past his class all the way to class C, where I was headed, and the whole time I could feel his stare right on my face.

I was trembling, here was this cool guy, my crush, finally noticing me, *internally screams*. When we got to the classroom, our class teacher was unfortunately already there and so they had to, unfortunately, head back to their class and that was when I knew that things were about to get interesting for me that year.

A few weeks went by, and we would see each other around the school complex but hardly ever spoke to each other, until one random day, as I was coming from the school cafeteria and he was on his way there, I "bumped" into him(well, not physically but you get what I'm trying to say), I was so nervous, but he stopped me with a "Hi, you dropped something", when I looked down I had dropped some of my change from the purchase I had made at the cafeteria, so I bent to pick it up, wanting to walk away as soon as I could, but the conversation did not just end there, he turned and asked if he could walk me back to class, and I said yes, of course (ugh, am I that predictable?). On our way back, he introduced himself as Andile, and to my shock he was in the 10th grade, I know I said what I said, I thought he was in the 8th grade, okay, but it turned out that he had a younger brother who was his cousin, who was in the 8th grade and that was why he was hanging out with the 8th graders most of the time, and I mean I should have noticed, I saw him wearing a blazer on the first day and blazers are only worn by 10th graders, 11th graders and 12th graders, but that did not cross my mind at all, so, I guess we can conclude that I wasn't that observant. I introduced myself as Rilonde of course, we didn't speak about a lot, but we only spoke about where we came from, we spoke about his grade, the subjects he had chosen or the career field he had chosen and you know, the random stuff, but before you know it, the school siren went off and we had to part ways. As days and weeks went by, we would greet each other whenever we came across one another, we would share our food, this was a classic young love affair coming into play. Until one day, he sort of, kind of, gathered the liver (what I mean is confidence) to ask for my number, so that we could get to know each other more over the phone, and that was where the relationship began. We would speak for long hours on end, on the phone, through chatting, via phone calls, via SMS, you name it, until one day we decided to make our relationship official, people were obviously asking questions, my friends to be specific, they wanted to know what was going on between Andy and I, and so, we decided we were just going to give the people what they wanted, and that is the truth. My friends knew Andy and I were an item, but not everyone was happy with that relationship. The truth is, Andy had his player ways, he was charming and came from a very well-off family, so, a lot of girls would fall head over heels for him because he always came off as though he was flirting even when he wasn't. So, I had many girls hate on me because Andy was their dream guy and I had finally gotten the player to somewhat settle down, well, not in marriage but in a serious committed relationship. But that did not mean that Andy and I did not have problems, because as a result of all the girls that paid him the attention, rumours would spread about how Andy was cheating on me with multiple girls, but when I confronted him, he would deny that. Unfortunately, our relationship didn't last long after that.

Moving along to how my sexuality began, I can't tell you how it started, but I remember when it started, thus I can only approximate the years of when it all began;

So, it was during my early high school years, I was probably between the ages of 13 and 14, that was when I began to become physical, not physical as in "I am having sexual intercourse", where a phallus is penetrated into the vagina, no! But at the time, my kind of physical was kissing. Kissing was a big deal in high school, okay? We used to have a spot back in my high school in 8th grade where young girls and boys would go "smooch". There was an old office space that wasn't occupied as often by teachers and learners, and that was the spot where everything went down after school. As young as we were, we were pretty mischievous and got up to no good. Young couples would agree on a date when the actual event would occur, while other learners who had no "love lives", would be filled with the excitement of having to watch as everything unfolded on the date agreed upon. I remember a day when my then boyfriend "Andy", and one of his friends decided that they were going to smooch their girls, it was so scary for me as that was my first ever actual kiss, I did not know how to, and I didn't want to embarrass myself and "my man", so I practised kissing the wall. Of course I cannot say it wasn't helpful, neither can I say it was, but in the end, all I remember was my boyfriend smiling from one end of his cheek to the other, and I just knew that he was impressed, and he was sure to let me know.

For me, kissing was not as much of a big deal as it was for my peers, but because it felt like an accomplishment, for the boys more especially, I do not know if it was a test of compatibility or a show off to the other gents, of entitlement to their girl, but I felt that I had to do it with, or for my then "boyfriend". I put emphasis on the term boyfriend with quotation marks as it's quite interesting where that word developed from. Like a boy who is a friend should be referred to as a boyfriend, but funny how that very same word can also be used to describe a relationship that is quite "physical & sexual", like where is the friendship there? Not that all relationships are just physical because for me relationships should have the following three elements to them, one being friendship, two being romance and three being partnership. And that is why I have reached a point at this age(my twenties), in this time, where I can only refer to someone I am attracted to more than just platonically, as a "partner"; a sexual partner, a life partner and/or even my person.

Intimacy as you might be aware is not just the state of being physical with somebody. Intimacy is the involvement of two souls in a spiritual act, it is the merging (more like a concoction) of various emotions, a truthful, yet vulnerable act. It is openness and transparency. Intimacy is allowing oneself to be illuminated by another's light, allowing them to see parts of you that only those who can come close enough can see. Intimacy is reaching within the depths of one's soul, by one or by another.

And that is how my "sexuality" began. With me being quite an emotional Being, kissing for me wasn't just an exchange of saliva, with the pulling of tongues, and a bit of biting of the lips, instead, it was intense. I did it with so much passion because that's exactly what I am – a passionate Being who puts their emotions into every single thing they do. Kissing came with this arousal, a sexual kind to be specific. It wasn't just a smooch, it came with the want to be touched, to be fully felt, not just physically, but elsewhere. It was a soul connection. The breath underneath exchanged with every touch, was symbolic of an evocation of emotions, of how deep my emotions ran. And that was the beginning of the addiction-pornography.

It started on a random day while I was surfing through the internet, back in the day I used to download music off some dodgy websites, as it was easy access and of course, free. And every time, I would come across "Ads" that were way too provocative, sexually. The age limit or restriction in South Africa for activities considered "illegal" ends at 18, and I was definitely underage at the time. Although the site required "confirmation or consent" that the person making use of their services was above the required age, i.e., 18, there wasn't any strict regulation or tight security that would have prevented anyone below that age from accessing the site, thus it was as easy as a "yes click" to the question " Are you above the age of 18?", for someone like me at the time (underage) to kickstart or contribute to their addiction.

From the title "dark-skinned man fing a brunette", to "Xxx videos", I was hooked. I would watch the videos and get aroused to a point where I wanted the feeling for myself. I began following what was done in the videos, to my own self, touching my own body, it would feel good for a moment, but the satisfaction would only last for a while, thereafter, the guilt would kick in, what does God think or say about this? Sexual immorality? The feeling of uneasiness would sink in every time. "I'm so sorry Lord, forgive me for this immoral act, I just want to stop, but the urge overwhelms me always", and the next time it happened, it would be a recital of the very same prayer. But it wasn't until one faithful day, that I took that active step to release myself from that bondage, it had to be done, it was about time that happened, but the temptation never went away, I guess I got stronger at denying my urge.

Pornography is surely addictive, and it is shameful to admit that you are struggling with it because people do not understand the extent of the effect pornography can have on an individual and might wonder "why don't you just stop?", so, allow me to give you a little insight on what pornography entails and what it does to a person.

Pornography is a pull towards a form of entrapment, to lose one's self-control as it traps your thoughts with images, sounds, and ideas that will lead you to act and think in a manner that you wouldn't necessarily act or think in, were you in your right senses. Pornography, like a substance, intoxicates you, and like a poison, it is a disease that affects your mind by playing games and implanting ideas that aren't any good for you. It is instant gratification, the entertainment of it, that is. Enjoyable for a short while but its effect is long-lasting and can take a while to get over, but even so, that does not mean that it is impossible to recover from, but once one is trapped, it can affect the way in which they act, a lot, resulting in them ending up forcing themselves onto someone else once they feel the urge to do the deed, and because it takes over one's self-control, one might just not be able to resist the temptation.

And we obviously cannot talk about pornography without touching on masturbation, the two cannot be separated, because once you see, the images, and sounds are transferred to your brain, the brain is a very powerful part of the human body, did you know that a lot that happens within, and externally from the human body, all begins up there? In the brain, yes. Take this for example; you get burnt while cooking food on the stove, actually no, you probably don't even like cooking, but let's just say you hit your small toe on the corner of a sharp-edged table, where do you think the pain is first registered? From your toe? Well, you got that wrong, the brain is where it all starts, there is a circuit where all data and information that goes on in your body is transmitted or transferred to your brain, then back to your body, so the minute you kick the table, your foot sends a message to your brain to say "hey, did you feel that? Is it painful? If yes, to what degree? Do we need to scream, kick or just give an ouch response and keep it moving?", then the brain receives that message and says, "well, looking at how sharp-edged that wooden table is, I must say toe, we got really hurt, look at the blood that's about to flow out of your toe, we have to make a scene, if you can, throw yourself on to the ground and scream like a hyena", the message is then received by the little pinkie toe, and yeah, we definitely feel the pain, it's extreme, unbearable, and we give the reaction as per the brains instructions. But what happens when the brain is contaminated just a little. A normal brain would look at a man or a woman and see just that – a woman and a man, but a brain that has a spike of pornography in it? It looks at a fully dressed woman and sees an x-ray version of her, it can already start analysing how her chest looks, how the well of her soul between her two pillars meant for balancing and carrying the upper body may look, it sees beyond just that, and it gets triggered, I'd like to touch that or feel that, or even see that, but because you can't just do that, we live in a world where people have rights and you wanting to do as you please without the consent of the other party, constitutes a violation to that individual's rights, so what do we opt for? Masturbation. But some people look at this as a way of self-exploration, exploring one's body, pleasing oneself, satisfying one's need, and I am not judging. We all have different views on sex and pleasure, and I guess everyone is entitled to their own opinions about it, but here's my take on it, based on my own personal beliefs, and hopefully those who share the same sentiments with me can relate and resonate with this; One thing I have noticed about this act is that because you are able to "satisfy" yourself, it can affect the way in which you experience sex with a partner. It may feel boring when they cannot read your energy, when they cannot understand your needs without you having to communicate to them, and that can feel very disappointing. When I think of sex, I always just picture two individuals engaging in that act, an act of pleasure and connection, and masturbation just feels like it is a mechanism to take all that away. But one could argue, well, what is so wrong with pleasing myself and connecting with myself, exploring the ocean, or well of my soul? Good question. But sex was never intended for that. What was is it intended for; you ask? If we take the time to look back to the beginning, life was simple, before the developments, life was easy. I would like to imagine that life or sex rather, was for the extension of mankind, sex was for reproduction purposes, for copulation, but also, sex served as an agreement, an agreement between two souls to come together, unite and become one. But you see change, although scary, can be good. Change introduces excitement, adventure, and brings forth imagination into the real world, but let us not forget that there is a good and bad side to everything. Where bad exists, there too exists good, it has since been the flow of life. So, change can be good, but it can also be risky and damaging, overtime. And sometimes we don't realize until it is too late or until we are far deep into it. Do you ever sit and wonder how the world started, and if everything you have ever heard or read about, were just theories? But of course, you do, do you sometimes wonder if we may have somewhere along the line, messed up with the flow of life? That maybe life was meant to be simple, and not as over complicated as it may be right now? Perhaps we were made to enjoy the simplicity of it, but then again, we could never escape the evolution of mankind, could we?

CHAPTER 8- THE ENCOUNTER

According to my grandmother, he was a commendable young man, one who valued family more than anything, respectable by & respecting to the community.

I remember the encounter just like it happened yesterday. It was during the festive seasons where he had lost his wife, she had suddenly fallen ill and passed away a few weeks after being diagnosed with ESRD(End-stage renal disease) also known as Kidney or renal failure. She was such a genuine soul, my grandmother worked for the family as their helper, and she spoke highly of her. She was kind and had even started an initiative for young women to confidently walk in their power in business, to grow and succeed, and I was fortunately, one of the young ladies who were granted the opportunity to work closely with her.

Many were affected by her passing and showed up to her burial in numbers to bid her farewell and show support to the family. I too were there, as I was close to the family because of the relationship my grandmother had with them. I was pretty close with their two daughters, Anzani and Roanda, and so the day after the funeral, Anzani, the eldest daughter, who was about the same age as me, 20, asked that I leave with them to the City just to keep them company as their father was supposed to return to work in the City and also, because I was supposed to be returning to College soon. And so, I spoke to my grandmother about it, and although she was hesitant at first, she eventually agreed to the idea and allowed me to leave with the family to the city, after all, they kind of were like family to us.

I slept over at the family's house the Saturday and Sunday evening. The day following Sunday, which was on a Monday morning, we woke up and drove to the city, it was a fun experience where we were blasting the speakers, jamming along to some great music. As soon as we got to the townhouse they were staying at, the girls decided that we were going to go out to get some food for us; dinner, as we were exhausted and didn't have the energy to prepare some. I, on the other hand however, decided to take a warm bath upstairs in the bathroom before we could leave, which was a room separate from the toilet, but during the time I was taking a bath, the girls decided to go out to get something for us, as I was taking too long, so they said. I was left behind when the girls went out, and I guess I was left alone in the house with him, Mundalamo. Because the next thing I heard while I was in the water was the swing of the bathroom door and lo' and behold stood Mundalamo at the door. I reacted with a shocked but embarrassed face, I was lying in the bathtub, relaxing my entire body against the tub, so I immediately sat up, covering my breasts with the face cloth I was using, when our eyes met, he turned back, immediately shutting the door, and apologizing for the invasion of privacy. Apparently, he had thought that I had left with the girls to get dinner. He used the toilet instead and went downstairs to get some work done. When I was done taking a bath, I wrapped myself in a towel as I left the bathroom, entered the guestroom that I was sleeping in, and shut the door closed.

The next thing I heard was a knock on the door from Mundalamo, asking that I borrow him my laptop, as he needed to finalize some work stuff on his company's website, but his laptop was not working or just something about the internet being bad. I wasn't, however, entirely dressed, as he demanded that I give the laptop to him immediately because what he was busy with was urgent. I looked for my laptop which was in my black suede laptop bag with a rose gold zipper, which was on the side table of the bed, and made my way to the door where Mundalamo stood waiting for me, I slightly opened the door handing the laptop over to him, when he asked for the charger, and I had to make my way back to the side of my bed to get it, he walked into the room, looking around, "you are a very well put together young lady", he complimented me. "Thank you", I responded. He continued talking, "you must be really tired from today's drive, I know that I am, we had a really long week, with funeral preparations and the packing thereof, I mean I know I could really do with a massage". I laughed, but not so loud and not too long, but just for the sake of disguising the awkwardness that I felt, I thought he was joking. I then handed the charger over to him and he took it while he made his way onto my bed. "Please take a seat", he said. I sat on the bed across from him, as there were no chairs in the room. "I've been meaning to say this to you; I am grateful for the support you have shown my girls, it really isn't easy for them, their mother's passing, but you keep them smiling"(Mundalamo speaking). It's no big deal, you know, I'm just doing what any friend would, I responded.

We went into a dialogue;

Mundalamo: **"But at least let me give you a massage as a token of my appreciation, you must be tired from the weekend."**

Rilonde: *Uhm, thanks but I am not feeling tired. Taking a bath really helped loosen up my joints and release the strains from my muscles, so I'm good, but thanks.*

C'mon, it's really just a back rub, that's all it will be, it won't even take minutes.
I am not a fan of massages, so I will pass, thanks! I replied.
C'mon, it won't take long, I promise, it's just a massage, nothing more. He insisted.

I was beginning to get annoyed and irritated over the whole setting and him begging me to allow him to give me the massage, but I think more than anything it was the confusion and fear of 'what is really going on here' that got to me and so I caved in and allowed him to give me the massage. He ordered me to sit right between his legs as he spread them wide open for me to sit. I went over and sat right where he had ordered me to, it's weird how I allowed myself to oblige to his commands because personally? I don't think that if I was in a good space in my head, I would have allowed that to happen. Perhaps I was just too naïve that I didn't want to notice the red flags my intuition kept flagging in front of me. He began to slowly, yet gently, rub his hands on my back, grabbing the flesh between my neck and shoulders the very same way you would give someone a back massage. I reacted, with a shiver from my upper body. **"What's wrong?"**, he asked. *I don't feel comfortable with this,* I said. He then told me to relax, said that he was not going to, in any way, do anything stupid, "Relax Baby, I won't hurt you" are the words that stuck with me.

I shut my eyes closed because it was at the moment that I knew what was going to happen next, and I knew not what to do or how to react. Mundalamo proceeded by inserting his tongue into my ear, it was a wet feeling that I got, and his breath was right on my neck, I got yet another shiver down my spine but this time it was fear, I was scared, is he going to do more than just this? But amid the fear, I felt numb, not just physically, but emotionally. He loosened the towel that I had my body wrapped up in, grabbed my breasts, rubbing his fingers against my nipples, I wanted to tell him no, stop, I don't want this, but it was as if I had turned into his little puppet. I couldn't, I could not get myself to say no. So, he stood up and pushed me onto the bed commanding me to sleep on the other side, and so, I scooped over and covered my naked body with my hands and legs, I was in a "knees bent, hands over knees, face buried in between arms and chest, sleeping on one side" kind of a position, when I felt his weight on the bed, he held the back of my head with one hand, bending it towards the object he held with his other hand, I had my eyes closed the whole time, but opened them immediately when I felt an object being forced into my mouth, but I did not keep them open long enough, I shut them immediately when I realized that he was trying to force his genitals into my mouth, I shook my head sideways "mm mmm, mm mmm", that was the only form of vocabulary that my lips and tongue could produce.

I wanted to cry so bad, so loud, but my ocean had dried up, my emotions felt caged, there was none to express, or I just didn't know how to at that moment in time. He then held my chin up to his face, and told me to look at him, as I opened my eyes, he said "it's okay, you don't have to put it all the way in", taking my hand and putting it right "there", telling me to "play with it", I- I didn't know how to, I mean, I have never found myself in this position before, in a situation like this and I just, I didn't want to. "I wish he could just say it was a prank, that he'd get up, dress up tell me to look at the camera over there in some hidden corner, laugh it out and leave me alone", I said to myself in deep thought. But that wasn't going to happen, this nightmare was my reality, and it was far from over. And so, I held it in my hand and rubbed it back and forth, but he just wasn't satisfied, I could feel it in his energy. He asked if I was still a virgin, I nodded, he then told me not to worry, that he'd "teach" me, and that "it" would be fun, and so he got off the bed and went to the end of the bed where my feet were hanging. I had my legs closed together, but he swung them wide open, proceeding with his tongue right into the well of my soul, he rubbed the labia majora together with the labia minora of my lotus and continued to insert his fingers inside of me, I squirmed just a little, it was uncomfortable, scary, what was happening, really just disgusting!

Was I being raped?

As already mentioned in chapter 6 titled "The rape Capital";

Rape, as defined by the South African Police Services(SAPS) is "The penetration, no matter how slight, of the vagina or anus with any body part or object, or oral penetration by a sex organ of another person, without the consent of the victim, it is the intentional, unlawful sexual intercourse with a woman without her consent. Sexual intercourse includes the penetration of the labia majora (outer lips of the vulva) and not just the labia minora".

So, I believe I was, being raped. He had not asked me whether I wanted to do this with him or not, I had expressed to him the fact that I felt uncomfortable with the whole situation, but what he did instead was to brush off my feelings like they did not matter and continued to seek the pleasure that he so desperately desired, from me, his helper's grandchild. He is old enough to be my father for crying out loud.

I squirmed in pain, letting out just enough sound to make him notice that I did not want that, what he was doing, and I did catch his attention, stopping the insertion of his fingers inside of me, he gave me a "what's up?" look, and asked "are you okay?", "Is this okay?", I then shook my head sideways, "mm mmm", replying to him. I mean, it was an obvious no, but he wasn't going to stop, because my "not wanting to, or not feeling okay about that whole situation" just wasn't a good enough reason to stop him from receiving the satisfaction he had planned on receiving from me, and so, he told me to "relax" instead, said that he wasn't a rapist, that he didn't intend on hurting me, that all he wanted was to have fun, and that that which was happening at the moment was fun, he promised not to go "too deep" because he didn't want to hurt me, I didn't understand what he meant there for a minute, but the sharp pain I felt next, explained exactly what he meant, he inserted his phallus into my vagina, it was slight; the insertion, but it came with a lot more force than the insertion of the previous "object" which he had used to penetrate me, that is his fingers. I felt it and all I could do was to hold on tightly to him, wrapping my arms around his upper body as he leaned onto me, I wanted to cry, but I couldn't.

So, I just laid there and watched the raindrops hit the ground as it poured with thunder & lightning, it was raining outside. I was truly scared of the sound that came with the rain, I wondered, has he done this to his daughters before, or to anyone else? If not, then, would he? Especially now that his wife- their mother, is deceased? Could he hurt his little girls? But my biggest concern or worry was "why me?", what was the necessity of this whole situation? Why did it have to happen on this day and why, why me? I wondered if God was right there, I knew he was! I- I knew He was looking over me the whole time, But I wondered why He let it happen, the rape, to me? I was frustrated, a little, "I thought You were supposed to watch over me, to look out for me, but just not this way", is all I could think to God.

He suddenly stopped jerking me, and came over to the other side of the bed on which he was sleeping, got onto the bed and asked that I give him a "tongue-licking on his genitals", of which I did, unwillingly because I felt I had no other choice, he then proceeded to kiss my lips, gently, and then demanded that I kissed him back because he "needed to ejaculate", I did, passionately so, because in my head what that meant was that this entire experience would be over soon, that he was finally going to let go of me, and that's all that really mattered to me. As I kissed him, he held his genitals with his one hand and kept rubbing it back and forth but more, in an up and down motion, you get? "Ahh, yes Baby, C'mon, that's it" he repeatedly said, calling out my name. I was shocked when he mentioned my name, he even made a nickname out of it, "Londi" is what he called me, I was disgusted, to the core of my stomach, sickened! He clearly was aware & conscious of what he was doing, and he just didn't care or find that awfully wrong. He then stopped and pushed me off of him when some liquid began to spill out of his genitals, that was his semen I guess, he was well pleased, I could see it written all over his face.

He got up and sat up straight on the bed while watching me, so I reached for the throw that was at my feet, where he was seated, ensuring that I made no eye contact with him and covered my body. He looked at me and laughed, asking for "something to clean up the mess", referring to the semen that was still very much spilling out of his genitals, the nerve! I pointed out my finger to the towel I had used to wrap my body with after that bath I had taken, it was on the bedroom tiled floor, so, he got up, picked it up, and wiped away the semen from his body. He covered himself with the towel, well at least his lower body, and sat there staring at me, he asked me how it was, like are you kidding me? This was not some fling you and I had, like no Sir, this was rape, and you know that too, so how dare you ask me how it was? Too bad I could only think that but not outwardly express it, so all I did was look at him without uttering a word, he then assisted me by asking if it was boring, if he was boring, and guess what? As much as I could not get myself to physically wipe away the smirk on his face as he asked me that, I was surely going to get on his nerve by nodding my head, as a "yes" response.

Oh, how disappointed he was, I could see that smirk fade away slowly from his face, and that for me was a victory. He received a call, he picked up, and while he was busy on his phone all I did was stare at the ceiling, absent-minded. **Londi...,** He called out to me, although I heard him, I did not respond, I guess my mind just wasn't there, **Rilonde...,** He called out again, I then shifted my focus from the ceiling back to him, he was done with his call. Hmm? I responded. Are you okay? "Mm" was the only answer I gave to him. He said he did not like the fact that I wasn't talking to him and threatened to sleep with me again if I didn't say something. He then got up and dressed, commanding that I do the same, which I did, I tried to cover my body with the throw just because I didn't want him to see me naked, but he grabbed the throw and threw it on the floor, laughing, **"C'mon, let me help you with your bra"**, clipping the back of my bra together. He came closer and kissed me on the neck, "I'll be right back", leaving me only to return with a R200 note, this is for you, buy something for yourself. All I could think was "am I just an object which men get to use or access whenever they please and pay for my services? Is that where he's trying to get with this? Is that what this is?" I was annoyed to my very core, but I didn't say anything, I looked at the note on the bed, looked at him as he left, saying **"I'll see you when I get back"**.

I made the bed and went over to the bedroom window, watching him drive out the gate. I then went to the bathroom to bath, again. I wanted nothing to do with him, I thought taking a shower would help remove all that disgust and shame I felt, so I scrubbed my body, as hard as I could, leading to me shedding so many tears, I cried so hard, I couldn't help but let it all out. A few minutes later the girls came back, I heard the door open and their voices in the lounge downstairs, I quickly wiped my tears away and dried my body, with a different towel, the other towel that he had used to "clean up the mess" was stacked up in the laundry bin in the guestroom that I was sleeping in. The girls came upstairs to my room and couldn't find me, but I bumped into one of the girls, Roanda, as I was leaving the bathroom going to my room, "wait, are you only finishing now with your shower?", she asked. "I mean, it's been long since we left and I believe we left you in the bathtub, isn't that so?"

Uhm yes, you're right! I, I had forgotten to wash my hair, you know, uhm from all the smoke and dust from the weekend, so I thought it'd be best to just jump in the shower instead and wash my hair.

Anzani jumped into the conversation "Oh, okay cool, Where's dad?"

Uhm, he left...

"Oh, yeah, he did say we might not find him by the time we get back home, he's got some work to do. Come let's go eat, we bought pizza!!"

We went to the lounge after I had finished getting dressed, to have dinner. As we were watching TV, Roanda looked over to me, to ask a question, "why didn't you just use the bathtub instead to wash your hair, because you literally just washed your entire body again? Or did you just want to try out the shower? Your hair isn't even wet though." We laughed it out as I tried as hard as I could to convince her to not make such a big deal out of it.

Mundalamo did not return home that evening. The morning of the next day, I woke up to go to my apartment where I was staying with my sister, and that was the last time I saw him.

CHAPTER 9- THE USE OF WORDS TO TRY AND EXPLAIN

Trust

Trust, I trusted him. He was never what I expected he'd turn out to be. I was so naïve. When he asked that I open the door for him, my conscious kept nudging me, as though it was giving me warning signs or signals of the danger that lay ahead. But I ignored the signs and kept telling my conscience to shut up when it kept giving me warning signs about him, only because I thought I could trust him. I just wanted to give him "the benefit of the doubt", because somehow deep down inside I still believed that there exist Beings with genuine intentions and not so much of a messed-up mindset. But can you blame me? He looked nothing like a monster. He was so gentle with me, he in no way had ever tried to be aggressive with me, but I guess the bad guys always put on a disguise, like the Sheep in "Red riding hood" who turned out to be a wolf, the big bad wolf. And perhaps for the longest time most of us never comprehended the message behind that story regardless of the many times we watched it because it literally was conveying a message of the kind of messed up world we live in, and all the while we thought it was just a fun film to watch. But I guess no one could have ever prepared me for such an unfortunate event because despite my mother having warned me about strangers, this was no stranger to me. There existed some form of familiarity between my perpetrator and I, I held him dearly to my heart, he was sort of like family. Although I was aware of the statistics of victims of such an assault, I, however, due to my imagination of the kind of scenery, time, and individual I always envisioned it would happen at/with and that is; somewhere in the streets, late at night while I was walking home, wearing a short skirt and a top that left out a bit of cleavage on my chest(although I have fairly small boobs), but I just did not foresee this happening the way that it did. And because this is so much like death, you can have a funeral cover or life policy in place, but you will never know at which day and time it will occur, no matter how much of a cautious life you lead, one can never prepare themselves emotionally for any loss accompanied by pain.

Reassuring

Reassuring, He was. He kept telling me that he would never do anything stupid and kept saying that I should trust him, and me being so trusting, I did, I trusted him. I mean he kept saying he was in no way a rapist, and so I reassured my conscious self that this same guy I feared would rape me would never do such a thing. And so, I gave myself;

"5 Reasons to Why He Wouldn't Rape Me"

#1 He's Christian. Well, His father is a Pastor of some church my grandmother and his family go to, back at home, and not to put any pressure on him because he's a PK A.K.A "pastor's kid", but I have heard him play a few gospel songs and he really enjoyed singing along. I have heard him quote a few Bible verses trying to get his point through to me. I've seen him post scriptures from the Bible on his social media, I think he believes in God. There is no way he would do something as horrendous as this. He is fully aware that it is wrong. He must know that "no means no" whether explicitly stated or expressed via body language.

#2 He's quite an intellectual guy. He's smart, okay? I know that pretty well. He works hard and as much as his life might not be where he wants it to be, he has done well for himself, in terms of his financial stability, so why would he risk it all just for a sexual connection with me? I believe he is smart enough to make the right decision, and that is to let me be if I were to try and express that I didn't want this.

#3 He has got little girls. He must know how it feels to have someone hurt a female close to you and you not being around to protect or defend them. He loves his baby girls and I bet he would be ready to break any guy's bones were he to try to hurt or cause them heartache. You know how older brothers or fathers can be towards their little sisters or daughters - overly protective.

#4 He is way older than me, and although age is just a number, I expect him to be mature enough to be able to distinguish between what is moral and immoral, sensible, and insensible. He cannot give any excuse as to why he would do something as horrendous as rape, he isn't under the influence of any substance, well unless there is a spiritual substance that would have suddenly taken control over him. But he is in his right senses, okay?

#5 We have just come from burying his wife a couple of days ago, give the poor guy a break, he is probably still grieving and has no time to be thinking of engaging in any sexual acts, especially not with a family friend, you are practically family.

And so, reassured I was, by him and by myself. That I became even more naïve, I literally fell into that trap, which was already set for me, it is like I somehow had just added paraffin to a fire that I, myself had not started, all in the name of trust. I knew deep inside that what was happening was so wrong, something that I did not want, but because of his reassurance, because of the trust I had towards him, I let him in, into my soul, without willing. But disappointment was just a couple of alphabets away put together to form a word that cut inches so deep through this human fleshed heart and little did I know that he would turn out to embrace this act of disappointment so much so that it would end up bruising me, I did not want to believe that he would hurt me.

Sexual

Sexual, he became. He began to fondle with every part of my being that I had believed for so long to be sacred. He slid his hands right under the towel I had covered myself in, he began to rub his hands all over the two cushion-like, almost-round, almost-saggy dairy producers on my chest. He was so close to me that I could feel his breath heavily on my neck, and he just wouldn't stop. I tried to tell him no, that I did not feel comfortable with what he was doing to me, in fact, I explicitly stated that to him, verbally! But he just brushed it off like it was nothing, like my feelings meant nothing to him, like they surely weren't about to get in his way of receiving satisfaction from a connection he was trying to have with this Feminal being, and yet again; he reassured me that it was okay, that it wasn't his intention to hurt me and to prove that, he said that wouldn't penetrate his fingers and phallus too deep through my labia minora, and into my vagina, but none of that made his actions right.

Defenceless

Defenceless, I laid there with my head facing the ceiling, having nothing left in me to fight him off, thinking to myself "I wish I had done something like physically attacked him, perhaps he would have seen that I really did not want to in any way engage in any sexual act with him", but I didn't. I just let him because I was too scared to say anything, I was too scared to defend what was mine, what he felt so entitled to, so instead of fighting back or fighting him off, I let him. I let him have his way with me, I let him get the pleasure he so desired from me, and he surely did. But I regretted every minute of my silence, I still do. I wanted to scream so bad, in hopes that someone would hear me and come to my rescue, but I just couldn't. I felt my throat lump up, my voice lower down, and my brain go flat, as I had no idea what I was going to scream out loud, "Do I scream 'rape'?", I thought to myself, "But he told me that it wasn't his intention to hurt me though", "I don't know anybody from this place, at least someone I can trust", thus silence became my only response.

He laid hold of every part of my being, not just the physical, but the emotional too. As he began to take and steal from me, I felt a part of me leave with him. He left my emotions caged. I could not utter a single word; it was as though I was in a separate sphere from him, like I was there but wasn't there. I could see the whole thing unfold right in front of me, like I was a separate entity from my body, I could see myself lying there, with the inability to disclose any emotion, and not because I was trying to come off as strong enough to take it, but simply because there was none to show. I was in so much shock that the whole experience felt surreal to me.

Bruised

Bruised, I was. I laid there after he had taken my sense of self from me. I just laid there with no sense of emotion left in me. I felt nothing. No anger, not even pain. No feelings. I felt numb and so defeated emotionally, that all my emotions felt caged and could not escape.

But pleased, he was with me. That he even said these words that have now for so long been replaying in my head "hmm, it must be nice being a woman hey?", till this day I do not understand that phrase/ question/ statement, I truly don't, because what does it mean, really?

CHAPTER 10- COMING OUT

My name is Rilonde, and this is my story.

I am a survivor of sexual assault (i.e., Rape).

Walking into the police station, crowded with men, I felt a little knot in my stomach, as I was reminded of what had happened to me, but I kept myself together, trying hard to not flinch. There were metallic benches right before the counters thus we made our way over there and sat on the benches as we waited to be attended to. I took a look around the room, it was super busy, filled with the voices of the police officers and other citizens who had come in need of assistance from our justice system. I relaxed my back onto the steel benches, but I felt quite uncomfortable in the way I was seated, so I moved a little closer to the edge of the bench where my knees were bent and I comfortably crossed my one leg over the other, and I put my right elbow on my knee so that I could balance my rested face on my hand. The staff at the police station were attending to each one of us according to who had entered the station first, when all of a sudden, a man walked into the station a few minutes right after we had just entered and began to cause chaos in the station, I was there with my sister (Remember I was in the city now, where my sister and I were staying in an apartment together, I told my sister what had happened a day after the incident and she suggested that we go report him to the police, because how dare he? What he had done was rape.), the guy had his shirt off and held it over his face to cover his bleeding nose, he had just come from a fight with another man, and for some reason, they had both agreed that it was best they went to the police to sort their matter out. It was quite interesting how they reasoned or had come to such a conclusion; I was quite impressed because I figured that had they dealt with it on their own, then one could've probably relocated and that's basically me saying 'ended up six feet under, in a grave at the graveyard'.

Although all the commotion that was happening in the station had shifted my mind off things a little, there was one particular individual who brought me back to the reality of things, of my situation. There was this young girl who had been there with her mother, I don't necessarily recall what it was they were there for, but I do remember that the conversation between the mother and the police officer included the words "affidavit" and so I believe it was nothing hectic that they were there for, well, unlike me. That young girl was still in her school uniform, she was wearing what they call a "Dungaree", which was a check kind of style with a combination of green, orange, and white lines, it came right above her knees. She wore that with her white socks and toughies shoes that had a little dust and I'm guessing that was from the busy day she had at school, she had her knitted green with orange and white lines on the wrist's jersey, hanging over her arm, right on top of the joint of where her elbow is situated underneath, and her hair was tied up in a bun to keep it all in place. I noticed all of these details about her because she was such a busy bee in that station. She kept moving around the station while her mother was busy with one of the police staff at the counter, and she did not necessarily sit in one spot while she waited for her mother to be done. I remember looking at her and thinking to myself "I pray you never get to a point in your life where you are robbed of your innocence" and I feel that was also triggered by the fact that that particular station was filled with so many men who kept their eyes on her, but at that point my judgement was a bit blurred out because of what I had just experienced, and so, I couldn't distinguish clearly between the look of "a hungry and thirsty predator watching its young prey" and the look of "this young girl has caught our eyes because she's such a busybody".

I had been sitting on those benches for close to half an hour and I remember feeling so emotional and overwhelmed by the whole situation, being in that station just solidified the fact that "it" had happened, it was as though reality had just kicked in and slapped me across the face and all I could do was tear up. I tried so hard to bottle my emotions and feelings, but just being in that place opened every wound. I felt a tingling sensation on my chubby cheeks as tears began to roll down my face, I tried to wipe them off but felt that every time I did, it was as though I was drawing attention to myself, and so, I stopped and just let them flow.

The gentleman at the counter called us over to assist us, when we got there, my sister tried to explain what had happened on my behalf, she told the police officer that I had been raped, and so the police officer told us to take a seat and that a female police officer would come to assist us. We waited for a few more minutes, then a female police officer approached the counter to take my statement, again, my sister tried to explain the whole situation on my behalf because I was tearing up, but the woman suggested it was best I gave the statement, "I do not know where to begin", that is what I told her, but she told me to just start anywhere. She then offered that we move to her office instead, as this was more of a personal issue, and we did. When we got to the office, I began to explain everything to her, from the burial to the travelling, to when the encounter occurred, I told her everything, she was so surprised at how calm I had gotten. After giving the statement she told me that I had to go to the hospital to a centre that deals with such issues, and to also take a rape kit. But she advised that I told my family what had happened to me.

A few minutes after waiting, we were told that a police car was waiting outside to take us to the hospital, we went out to where the car was parked and got into the car, and no, it was not a van, it was a car. Upon our arrival, I noticed two male police officers in the car, I was sceptical at first, about having two male officers drive a rape victim to the hospital, but I just went with it. They drove us to the hospital, to the Thuthuzela Care Centre, and left us to sleep there, as it was already late(around nine PM in the evening). We had gone late to the police station (at around five, half five PM), which explains why we arrived this late to the centre. To explain what the centre is all about, it is a critical part of South Africa's anti-rape strategy, with the aim to reduce the number of victims of rape, child abuse, and domestic violence, through prevention, response, and support for victims. The Thuthuzela Care Centre works as follows;

Firstly, you can report a rape case directly to a Thuthuzela Care Centre (usually based at community clinics or hospitals) or report to a police station, where you will be referred to the centre after opening a case with the police. Secondly, the staff at the centre will help get you immediate medical attention, counselling services at the centre will then be arranged for you, if you haven't opened a case as yet, then the staff at the centre will help you open a case and arrange for ongoing counselling and court preparations.

When we arrived at the centre, we received a warm welcome from one of the staff members at the centre, they had a lounge area where we were asked to take a seat and wait for their assistance. After a few minutes of waiting, I was called into an office by one of the staff from the centre and she explained how the medical examination would be conducted and what items of my clothing might be taken for evidence, for example, my underwear if necessary. We then proceeded to sign a consent form that allows the doctor or nurse to conduct the medical examination on me, and after that, I was directed to the examination room where a nurse was awaiting my arrival for the medical examination to be conducted. When I got there, she asked whether I had taken a bath post the incident, I replied yes, and she gave me this look that left me feeling as though she did not believe that I had been raped because "who in this century is still unaware of the guidelines/steps that need to be followed post-rape?". I wanted to let her know so bad that the only reason I had taken a bath was that I did not want any of his DNA left on my body, I felt dirty, and that was why I showered, I thought showering would get rid of all that shame I felt, I thought it would make me feel a little less blemished, but it didn't. And it's not that I wasn't aware that one is not supposed to take a shower before a rape kit is performed on them, and that is if they are going to open a case against their perpetrator, I knew that very well, but no one prepares you for the emotional confusion after such trauma, you hear about all these steps to follow if you were to find yourself in the situation, but when you are in it, your mind doesn't immediately think of those steps or guidelines and so, whatever I thought of doing then felt right, but also, it hadn't even crossed my mind; the thought of not taking a shower as a way to preserve his DNA as a form of evidence. But I brushed it off because "she is doing her job, her best, to try and help me".

She then asked for a bit of information with regards to what had happened, she asked whether he had penetrated through my vulva, into my vagina(we shall call her Vallerie), if so, with what, and whether he had used protection, whether I had a sexual partner, if yes, when last I had sexual intercourse. I answered every question as honestly as I could, I told her that he had penetrated with his fingers & phallus into my Vallerie, but not too deep and that he hadn't used a condom, I told her that I didn't have a sexual partner whom I was involved with and that I had never had sexual intercourse before the encounter, as I was still a virgin. She did not necessarily believe the part where I said I was still a virgin and I say that because of the remark she made; "we will see that when I conduct the test", I got scared a little because to be honest, as much as I had never slept with anyone before, as much as I had never had a phallus penetrate through my Vallerie, that did not necessarily mean that I was innocent, because I had explored certain parts of my well with my fingers, but did that mean that I was excused from the "still a virgin" category?

After our conversation, she asked that I went to the bathroom to remove my clothes and change into the hospital 'robe' she handed over to me and asked that I urinated into a cup as a sample of my urine was needed to conduct the STD/STI/ Pregnancy tests. I did, as requested, and returned to the office, she then asked that I lay on the bed, as she was going to take a swab from my vulva and Vallerie in case some of his DNA was still there. I wasn't so comfortable with anyone going down there especially after what had happened, but I agreed as I felt that it must be necessary. She had a torch and some swabs and as she began to swab, she made a comment that disturbed me, "you are such a liar, you said you were not having sex, but I can tell by looking into your Vallerie that you are definitely having sex", I was so confused, like, how can one tell by just looking into someone's Vallerie that they are no longer a virgin? I have done some research and there is no way one can tell whether the hymen is still intact or not, a hymen is a thin, fleshy tissue that stretches across the opening of the Vallerie, but the hymen isn't really symbol as to whether someone is still a virgin or not, as it can be "broken" or lost through so many ways. Some women are born with very little hymenal tissue, which makes it seem as though they do not have any, while others lose their hymen in the gym where the hymen stretches and breaks apart during intense workouts or exercise, some people lose their hymen as a result of using tampons, whereas other people lose their hymen through riding a bicycle, and how you would know that the hymen has been stretched or broken; is through light bleeding, varying between individuals with how strong their hymenal tissue is, whether it's small, very thin or thick, and so, having sexual intercourse isn't the only way a hymen can be "broken", and that is why a man could have sexual intercourse with a woman who has never had sexual intercourse before and still not experience bleeding. Virginity is a really tricky topic as many people hold different opinions on what it means, but the basic definition of virginity would be; never having had sex before, but it would be ignorant for me to stick to only that definition of vaginal penetration as we have other individuals who, for them, sex is different, ranging from oral sex to finger penetration. However, at the end of the day, you are the one who gets to decide whether or not you are a virgin. But also, why do we only look upon women to see if they are still "intact", what about the men?

When she was done with swabbing and taking samples of my blood for my HIV/AIDS test, she asked that I go change into my clothes, and I did. When I returned to the office, she explained that I would be notified after a few days of the results of my tests. She proceeded to explain that I would need to take antiretroviral drugs, which will assist in preventing any virus from spreading in the case where my perpetrator is infected, and that is only because we were not aware of what his status was. She explained exactly how I needed to take the medication and wrote everything down for me, she gave me an appointment letter with a date, which I needed to come with when I returned to collect my results and told me that I would also receive counselling from the centre on the specified date. After that, I was free to leave, but because it was already late, we were offered a room to sleep in at the centre and were notified that a police officer would come to pick us up on the morning of the following day. Honestly, I couldn't sleep through the night, I kept replaying the whole event in my head, I kept thinking of how it had happened, and why it had happened, I just wanted to dig a hole for myself, crawl in, never to come out, especially because I still had my family to tell the story to.

It was the morning of the following day, when a police officer arrived in a police van to take us back home, the investigating officer was supposed to have a word with me but she had not pitched yet, so the police officer drove us back home and a few minutes after the drop off, another car drove to the gate of my apartment, it was the investigating officer, she gave me a call to come open the gate so she could come through, of which I did, she used the lift to my apartment and got to my place, I welcomed her in, my sister left to go to a friend's flat, just to give us that privacy, the officer asked that I repeated my statement to her, just to confirm that they had captured everything and that no information pertaining the incident had been left out and we simply went through my statement again, after that, she received a call from the other investigating officer who is in charge of the forensics, we had to go to the scene to take pictures, and so, I called Roanda and asked if there was anyone at home, and whether her dad was there, she agreed to being home but responded with a "no" to her father being around, and so we sent the forensics guy the address and drove off to the house, once we arrived, the female officer went in and explained to the girls what had occurred, and what we were there for, the girls couldn't believe it, they were shocked and began to burst into tears, I couldn't bear to watch them, being there made me feel some type of way, the thought of how he could just walk in to the house at any minute and I don't know what I would do or how I would react, I was truly scared.

The forensics guy took pictures of the scene, although I had moved things around in the room, as well as pictures of the towel that he had used to clean himself up with, the officer thought that that could be used as evidence, after gathering evidence, the female officer then asked for his number so that she could call him and let him know of the situation at hand. I was shaking, scared, I did not know how to feel about that, she called, and he picked up, she shared everything with him and told him that he had to turn himself in, and he basically agreed to turn himself, we then left, and I got dropped off at my apartment.

A day after the case was opened, I received a call from my grandmother asking what was going on, because Mundalamo's eldest brother had shown up at her doorstep telling her about the rape, and that he was pleading that we please sit down and have a conversation as a family, that we could "fix" this, said that some families sit and come to an agreement to reimburse the victim through some form of payment and that there was no need to involve the police or the law. I was gutted to hear that, I mean, how dare he? But I tried to explain to my gran what had happened as difficult as it was, and she understood and was quite sympathetic with me, and that was how my family got to know.

I am not just a statistic! Yes, I got raped, but that does not make me only a fraction representing the number of people who have been unwillingly forced or coerced, and/or manipulated into having their bodies engaged in any form of sexual activity(s).

I may have survived a bodily-privacy invasion that was cruel and painful/brutal (maybe not so much physically but more emotionally), but I am not just a survivor of rape! I am a Feminal being, not weak, but gorgeous, strong, compassionate, and powerful.

I may have been too trusting to an individual who had the wrong intentions when it came to me, and took advantage of me, but I am not too soft and easily deceived and just too naïve. I have a way of always giving people the benefit of the doubt, a way of seeing the good in everything and everyone because everyone deserves to be trusted until they prove you otherwise, and that is my strength.

I may have lost my willpower, strength, and voice during the encounter, but that does not mean that I am weak. I was scared and shocked, so I froze, that is why I did not know how to react. And that's something that took me a while to figure out, I was angry at myself for so long for why I did not fight him off, "why didn't I bite him, or push him off?", I've asked myself quite a lot of times, but it wasn't until I ran into an article on our friendly assistant "Google", explaining what exactly happens during the actual Rape encounter. Now, according to this article, it's stated that one of two things can happen during Rape, and those are the flight or fight mode, which are very much self-explanatory but allow me to elaborate further, just for your convenience.

Now, to begin with what "fight mode" is, fight mode can also be referred to as the "attack mode". For the victim, this is 'trying to defend yourself by fighting back', this entails actual physical violence to try and escape from the scene or to try to hurt your perpetrator in hopes that that will make them back off, or back down from assaulting you. Moving on to what "flight mode" means, according to my research, this is the most common of all responses to rape, for many rape victims, and many spend their lifetime angry, bitter, and blaming themselves for what happened, which I hope will be cleared by my explanation below;

The flight mode is more of a state of mind response, which leads to the physical response of what we call "freezing". What happens is that the victim, instead of physically fighting against their perpetrator, they flee. And what that means is that they escape from the reality of their situation. The victim becomes absent-minded from what is happening and to set the record straight, I am no psychologist and I do not know enough about the human anatomy or brain, that I can explain in as much detail, what exactly goes on in a person's mind during rape, but with the piece of information I've gathered and were able to piece together, it's most definitely based on how an individual has been programmed, so it depends on one's background, how one has always responded to difficult situations happening around them, which is basically how their response will be during rape or any other form of trauma. Take this for example, if you've always been one to back away from your problems and not face them head on, then you are most likely to go into the "flight mode" response during an incident such as rape.

On the other hand, if you've always been one to speak up and voice out your concerns then the fight mode will most likely be your response. But also, let's not forget that when we're faced with new challenges which require our immediate response, it can cause us to act in a way we wouldn't necessarily act had we been in the right state of mind, and that is "not scared or in shock".

Being Christian, I felt condemned a little, I wondered what God said about rape, what his view was on this topic, whether I was at fault as well. And so, I took it upon myself to do a bit of research in the context of the Bible, and this is what I found; I found that Deuteronomy 22:23-29 was the most referred to Bible verse when it came to seeking justice for victims of sexual assault.

And based on my research, this is what I found on the Internet:

Rape in terms of Biblical law, was viewed as an act of violence, in fact, it was no different from murder. In Deuteronomy, it is evident that the woman did not consent to the rape, she was helpless, and the man took control over her, therefore, her perpetrator was the only one found guilty and she, innocent.

As mentioned before, in cases of rape you may find that the victim is not able to defend themselves because they froze, meaning they were unable to move, scream, let alone understand why that was happening. A lot of these victims end up blaming themselves for not being able to defend themselves, as if it were their fault. Now, the bible places emphasis on consent, and in this case, the woman had not consented, meaning that she was taken advantage of, unwillingly.

I did further research to understand what was meant by "they froze" during a sexual assault and this is what I found:

According to my research, the brain contains what we call the amygdala, an important area forming part of the brain, which is responsible for producing responses when fear or threat is detected. Once the threat is detected by this area of the brain, the amygdala sends an alert to the brainstem to disable movement, which is how freezing occurs. Freezing is thus a response from the brain detecting any threat or danger that may lie ahead.

The response to a traumatic event like rape, depending on your brain's development and how you are used to responding to new, shocking experiences, can vary, leaving some individuals "frozen" and others being able to fight back. Some individuals experience what we call a feeling of numbness; where an individual experiences some fogginess in the brain and reality, and is thus unable to move or speak, whereas some pass out during the encounter and others suddenly burst into tears without knowing what to do or how to respond, and simply just give in. All this can result in a lot of self-blame for those who do not know or understand that these are only reactions of the brain. In fact, if we were to be more gender-specific, out of embarrassment and shame, men can choose to not disclose the fact that something as disturbing as rape happened to them, not even to their most trusted peers, as they are perceived as masculine and are expected to always fight back.

However, if it so happens that the victim of rape speaks out about such a case or incident, they often fall into a state of regret as the police officers taking the statement, college administrators they have reported the incident to, most trusted friends or family members, can think to themselves or even outwardly express "why didn't you fight back or scream?", and even with the inability to fight back or talk back, expressing that one does not want to engage in any sexual activity with another individual, that does not mean that consent was or is present, because our brains respond differently especially when induced with fear, and also, just because a victim does not remember everything, even the most important details of the scene, it does not mean that they are lying because our brains do tend to give memories that are not so complete, mainly because we may be trying so hard to shy away from and not go back to the parts of our memories that once broke us.

I wonder how my family feels about this. We often focus so much on the victim and how they are affected and forget that the relatives of the victim or anyone closely related to them are also affected by such traumatic events. They may not know how to respond to us when we share the news with them, let alone treat us(the victim) because this is also very much traumatising for them too. The people who I am worried most about, are my parents, they have spent so long trying to protect me from this, or anything worse than this and I can't imagine how disappointed they must feel, not in me but in themselves. My father must be feeling the guilt of not being able to protect his baby girl from being attacked by "a monster". My dad and I are pretty close. I can't say that I relate to many young girls who have grown up without having known their biological fathers or having had a relationship with them, because unlike them, I did. I grew up in a family that wasn't considered broken. And that is not to say that families with separated parents or single mothers as the parent are broken, because if we are being honest, you could have both parents living under the same roof, who just don't see eye-to-eye, and have another family with separated parents but who seem to be effortlessly co-parenting, or a single mother raising her kid fairly well, even after her baby daddy has left her and denied custody of the child. And so, exactly what am I referring to when I talk about broken families? These are families that aren't as peaceful, families with a toxic environment for kids to grow up in, such as but not limited to; households where individuals experience domestic violence, child abuse, and a lack of peace and harmony.

I'm such a homebody, so, the chances of me going out are quite slim, but on top of that I guess I could say that my father was a little strict. I did not really have a curfew, but that is because I was known to always be around at home, and going out even just during the day, to go meet up with "a friend", always came as a surprise to my dad. For some reason, he had assumed or concluded that I had no friends, because I hardly hung out with anyone. So, knowing something like this had happened to me must be dreadful for him, he knew I wasn't the troublesome type, and that I surely did not deserve such behaviour towards me.

The truth, like the sting of a bee, is always going to hurt. And I saw how his brother tried to defend him when he approached me to ask about the incident, although he didn't say much due to the shock of the news, he just couldn't believe that his brother would do such a thing. He drove to the city to bail his brother out, and while he was there, decided to meet up with me to apologise on his behalf. I could see it in his eyes, that he wanted to believe so bad that his brother hadn't done such a thing, that I was perhaps just a girl seeking attention, a girl seeking to break his family apart or ruin the life of his brother, which was sadly not the case. But that is what happens with a lot of people who are informed about this- rape. When you have known a person all your life, or for quite some time, you tend to become soft towards them and what I mean by that, is you develop this idea about who they are and you hold onto that, the closer you become with them, the harder it is for them to truly express who they are because of the fear of judgement. Because you see them as "perfect", they try in all ways possible to conceal their dark side from you, so as to keep up with this perfect image they have portrayed to you, but what you don't realize one bit is that we all have a dark side to us, and unless we're willing to shed light onto it, by revealing it to our most trusted circle, we consciously, slowly begin to fade away into that darkness, allowing it to consume the entirety of our Being. We continue to submerge ourselves in this darkness because we feel that there isn't anyone who will be able to listen and not judge, mainly because our deep dark secrets feel exactly like that - "Deep - Dark - Secrets". But what we fail to realize is that when the light illuminates the darkness, it exposes everything that was once hidden. Nothing is too dark for the light; the darkness cannot help but surrender to the light because with its brightness everything becomes renewed. One thing I believe that one needs to realize is that they should never put anyone on a pedestal, that just helps leave room for disappointment because nobody is perfect, they may appear to be, or you may just be blinded by what they put out for you and everyone else to see, or by their potential to be good, but the truth is; we all have our inner deep dark secrets or struggles that we keep only to ourselves.

Truth is as long as you are dealing with a creature that has feelings, emotions, opinions, beliefs, thoughts, and a personality or even multiple personalities, also referred to as a human being, you need to know that you will experience some form of disappointment in your dealings with them. Because the thing about humans is that we are imperfect, and we pride ourselves in that. We more than often fall short to temptation, we lack self-discipline when it comes to things that we know are so wrong; we just can't say no, we make mistakes, a lot of mistakes, because we are on a journey of learning, unlearning, and relearning. We know less than we think we do, hence, the mistakes we make. It's as though as humans we like to embrace this act of disappointment so much, it's like we enjoy inflicting pain onto one another and blaming it on the faults of being "human". But at the end of the day, the truth that remains is that we are no gods, we are humans and therefore no matter how much influence we have on other human beings, no matter how many achievements or possessions we have attained, we too are just human, and that is a realization that everyone needs to come to.

Oftentimes, when victims or survivors of any form of assault and even just heartache speak out, people tend to think that they are doing so because they are seeking attention or some form of sympathy or pity from those around them, but that isn't the case here; the only reason I'm speaking out about my traumatic encounter is that I want to be able to speak up for the ones who got killed before they could voice out their true version of events that took place, I want to stand up for the ones who, like myself, might think "IT WILL NEVER HAPPEN TO ME", but it does and because of the shame, and the fear of judgement, are afraid to share their story, and that is through sharing my story. I want to educate on what it really means and how it feels to experience and go through something like rape. I believe that my life is an attestation for someone out there and so, I want to do it for all the individuals who have been sexually violated but never got the justice they so deserved! I want to do it for my future sons and daughters, although that is a thought still to be pondered upon, as I sometimes feel unsure as to whether I want to be involved sexually and intimately with someone(a man), if I want to surrender my body to any man, after my "dignity" was forcefully stripped off of me. I think I'd feel ashamed to be butt naked around a man or anyone, to begin with. I feel it's going to be hard because it is not entirely easy to not feel like a raggedy old rug, lying on the floor, and dirty as hell. When your soul's been ripped apart, it can never be easy to feel the same way you did before "this". I do not know if I want to raise my kids in a world that is as tarnished as this world, we live in. I fear that I will bring my baby girl into a world that will steal her innocence away and expose her to things that she shouldn't be exposed to at an early age. I am afraid that although I will raise my son to have high morals and to hold an equal amount of respect for everyone out there, this lurking spirit that's been possessing our men, will find its way into his mind and heart and lead him to one day perpetrate such a gruesome act towards a young girl, or even an older woman, let alone another man!

However, the most important reason why I am speaking out is because I want to do it for myself. I am deserving of a lot of things that have happened to me, but I am undeserving of this.

So, I'm here to change the narrative. No longer will perpetrators look at victims and survivors of assault and think we are weak, that they have every right to strip our Dignity off us. I'm here to redefine the whole concept of how a "victim or survivor" should be acting after such trauma i.e., scared, ashamed, defeated, unworthy, or lifeless. Because I am fully aware of my truth. And as much as I have wanted to give in, let him see the piece of me he left with, I just can't. So, instead of shying away from this painful truth of having been a victim at some point, that I now must live with, I choose to reveal the woman inside of me, filled with valour, love, vision, life, faith, and purpose. I am a story yet to be told!

CHAPTER 11- TRIGGERED

As much as healing can take place in one's life, that does not mean that one can, and will never experience triggers, and well this was mine. Allow me to introduce you to Thabiso, well, in short, "Tee". Tee was a really fine wine, okay? He was just something else. Tee and I met in College, but that was not the first place that I had seen him before; I had met Tee back at our College's therapy centre, which was about two streets away from the College building, that was our usual spot to meet at, unintentionally though. I was doing my second year in College, studying Psychology(although I could not finish my studies that year, my brain was a train wreck), where he was also doing his final year but as a part-time student, as he had an internship that he was busy with at the school's Psychology centre. I used to go to the school's Psychology centre for my weekly meetings with one of the psychologists there. Tee was working or rather, doing the administration part of things, and I was a patient at his workplace. It was all professional, until I began to feel as though there was a vibe between us. I could feel the difference between how he spoke to me, and how he spoke to the other patients. With me, it was long "get to know each other" conversations, whereas with the other patients it was just pure business, no pleasure, whatsoever. But I could sense Tee get a little nervous whenever I was around him, I probably came off as intimidating for him because he had admitted to me that he thought that I had a resting bitch face, which didn't come as a surprise for me.

Tee was just alright when I first met him, no sparks flying whatsoever because at the time I met him, I was still battling with the trauma from my rape. And, because Tee was just holding back a little bit of his feelings towards me, or perhaps that was because I wasn't too open to the idea of anything happening between us on a romantic plane. I remember our first conversation, we spoke about where we come from, where we had gone to school, what we do for a living, and how come he had never seen me before because we were kind of from the same living area, were going to the same College, and had mutual friends, but had never been in the same circle, ever! How interesting that was. But the conversations weren't that alluring for me at the time, owing to the fact that I was still battling with my recovery from the trauma. Yes, you're right, Tee and I met after the encounter. So, I wasn't exactly looking into engaging in any ship, be it platonic, romantic, or acquaintance, I just wasn't interested, especially not with this other gender. I did not take him seriously at first, because I didn't want to open myself up to love without being sure of whether I was still hurting, or if I was healed. So, I held back a lot of my emotions and feelings, because of the fear that the trauma would occur again, and just because I felt men could not be trusted any longer. But as time went by, my encounters with Tee seemed to get quite interesting, and I sort of, kind of, started to like Tee, just a little.

Either way, the first time Tee ever tried to make a move on me, was when he asked whether I was seeing someone, I mean, why would anyone randomly just ask that question if there wasn't more to their asking? So, I told him "No", but he just wasn't buying it because "there's just no way that a pretty girl like you has not yet been cuffed to one gent", such a typical response from a guy, right? But, trying his luck, he asked if, and when I would be available, as he wanted to take me out on a date. I did not entertain that "friendly" yet "flirty" gesture, and we both kind of just let it slide.

A few months after our unplanned, unarranged meetings, Tee finally mastered the confidence to ask for my number. It was cute, okay? Tee and I had bumped into each other at College, randomly so, and that was when Tee and I started "talking". Yes, Tee and I had been seeing each other around his workplace(not dating), but Tee only finally mastered the confidence to ask for my number when we bumped into each other at College, he had tried before, to ask me out on a date, but I just wasn't budging. He even admitted to being a bit scared to ask for my number as he was trying to maintain the professionalism between us at his workplace, and didn't want to get into any sort of trouble at work, were I to report him and say that he was bothering me, harassing me, or anything of that nature, but he just could not help but want to get to know me further and speak to me whenever, and not just when I visited his work place for their services. And so, I gave him my contact details.

We started talking over the phone, constantly, and the reason for that was because Tee was busy juggling school and work, thus we couldn't hang out as much. He seemed interested, but things were moving rather too fast for me. Tee was such a fun spirit to be around, he had that inner child that he just wouldn't let die, or

153

perhaps he was just immature? But either way, that was one thing I liked about him. However, one huge thing that I picked up from Tee was that he struggled from some form of childhood trauma he just wouldn't confront, of which he used his "confidence" to try and conceal.

The truth about Tee was that he struggled with abandonment issues, and the best way to protect himself was through his bad boy tendencies. Tee never begged to be in a relationship, he would walk out as soon as he sensed that the relationship was becoming too serious, he feared rejection, and he feared being left out in the cold in a relationship that he would have invested so much into. But one thing that puzzled me the most about Tee, was that he had been in a previous serious relationship where he got burnt, with a girl he loved so dearly, and although that ship should have sailed ages ago, he was still holding onto dear life to that relationship. He never wanted to be open about what was going on in that situation because "it is too complicated for you to understand", he'd tell me. But I could sense that something bothered him from that relationship, however, he just wouldn't walk away from it, it was as though he was hooked, like a fish, and could not let himself loose. I guess his abandonment issues may have resulted in him developing co-dependency, or perhaps he felt that he just couldn't walk away from something that he had already invested so much into. Tee grew up with his aunties, from his maternal side of the family. His mother had fallen pregnant at a young age and had to go back to school after giving birth, to finish her studies, hence the inability to raise her son and care for him the way a child would require attention from his mother, whereas his father was also a very busy businessman. I believe that was where Tee's abandonment issues stemmed from because he officially only started being raised by his parents when he was a young teenager, around the age of 13. Although Tee had moved in with his parents to their new home, he wasn't staying with his mother and actual father, because his mother had been "re-married", since she and Tee's biological father had separated when he was at a very tender age. Although his stepfather treated him like his own son, Tee didn't have a strong bond or connection with his biological father.

Besides Tee's abandonment issues, egotistical behaviours, and flight mode tendencies - dissociation, he was a pretty chilled guy, but what bothered me the most about Tee, was the fact that he was half honest, and that just means that he was good at admitting things, but when it came to explaining himself? He failed, dismally! He wasn't transparent, and I could understand that that was probably because we were still in the beginning stages of our relationship, more like a 'situationship', but he wouldn't tell you something unless you confronted him about it, and even so, he would limit his answer to only what you had asked, nothing more. For instance, Tee and I got to a point where we were catching feelings for one another (well, I don't know if that was part of his agenda or not, but I doubt that it was because he had a girlfriend at the time), and I confronted Tee about whether he was in a relationship or not, and he said yes, but when I asked him what he wanted from me he said he wanted "love", which made no sense because YOU HAVE A GIRLFRIEND Tee, what do you want from me?? Let me give you more context as to how that whole confrontation panned out;

I don't know what happened, but I went from being not so interested in Tee, to being extremely interested in Tee, in what felt like split seconds. Perhaps it was the attention that I hadn't been receiving in a while that he was giving to me, that made me feel interested, or perhaps I thought I could feel safe around him after my encounter because he seemed genuine at first and made it seem as if he had no intention of causing me any pain or ache. I always got excited every time I had to go to his workplace, perhaps it was the attention I was receiving from him, just seeing him, and having our usual conversations made me happy. But when we started talking outside his workplace, I found him to be very funny, smart, super sarcastic, yet so gentle and loving underneath all of that sarcasm. Our first arranged meeting was a few weeks after we had exchanged numbers, make that three (3), to be exact. Thabiso picked me up from my place after work, and we went over to chill at his place, first thing I noticed about him? He was considerate. It was cloudy outside, perfect weather for coffee or tea, and I don't care if he was just craving the coffee himself, but the fact that he offered me some, makes me say that he was considerate. But from the first day I had an arranged meeting with Tee, I knew something was off about our connection, my intuition was just on another plane, and could sense all these things from far away.

After making the coffee, Tee came over to sit next to me, we spoke a bit, there was always laughter in our conversations, always, but one thing I could not ignore on that particular day, was this feeling I felt right before my encounter, there was something about Thabiso that reminded me of my perpetrator. They both were too confident in their sexuality, I guess, but it felt as though there was an ego issue there, that 'I'm better than everyone else and I get whatever I want' type of energy, I didn't like that I felt that way about Tee, but I buried the thoughts in some laughter, ignoring the red flag, and before you know it, Tee held the lower back of my head, almost to the side of my neck, and leaned in for a kiss. From his gentle, soft lips, to the slowness of the kiss, to how much passion it came with, that kiss was almost perfect, but it triggered something in me, the rape. I began to tear up, out of nowhere, you can imagine how embarrassing that was, and having to explain why I was crying? That was just not it for me. Poor guy though, for a minute there I bet he was so confused with what was happening, but I ended up explaining everything to him, that I had been a victim of rape and that the kiss was just a trigger, that that was my reason for crying. He seemed interested in hearing what had happened, and judging from what his questions were? He's a "fair" guy. He wanted to know whether the guy knew what he was doing. Although at first, I thought it to be a stupid question to ask, it was fair, depending on what grounds he was asking though, if he was asking whether the guy was intoxicated or not, it would be a stupid question because even if one is intoxicated, they would still know what they are doing, so that's out of the question. If he was asking whether something was going on between the guy and I, thus the guy only saw it fit to 'make a sexual move on me' because perhaps we're dating, it would also be a stupid question because "just because you are in a relationship with somebody, it does not mean that you are entitled to their body, you need to find out if they are okay with getting sexual with you, and if not, respect their decision", so you know what, let me take back my words and say, it was a stupid question. But I say he's fair in the sense that he wasn't quick to stand up for anyone, instead, he was willing to listen to the story and judge for himself, without any bias.

But that two-minute distraction of me tearing up, did not entirely shift his focus from the initial goal, and so he allowed me to cool down for a few seconds and then asked if I was okay, proceeding with what he had started. He surely couldn't keep his hands to himself, but eventually, we stopped before things could get too greasy. It was time for me to leave, when a small voice in my head whispered, 'ask if he is seeing someone', of which I did, and to my surprise, he said yes, with no shame whatsoever. I was hurt because what he was doing with me didn't make sense, I mean, what did he want from me when he was already with someone else? But he explained that he wanted to make me his, and that he wanted something serious with me, and that the ship from his relationship had already sailed. How naïve of me to want to believe him. It was from that answer that I knew I was going to get hurt if I allowed myself to fall for him. I left angry that night, I wanted absolutely nothing to do with him, I was disgusted with his behaviour, and I couldn't help but think to myself "men are all the same, they are all after one thing and that is not love", how unfair of me to think that way though. But of course, that did not stop me from continuing my pursuit of a relationship with him. I know you are probably judging me right now, like what are you doing with somebody else's boyfriend? But hear me out;

Because women are emotional, that makes us quite gullible and easily trusting, but that's no excuse. Thabiso called me right after dropping me off at my place, to "talk". He pleaded with me to not cut ties with him, at least not so soon, said that his relationship with his girlfriend wasn't as serious, and that we had just met, and he wanted me to give him a chance to prove himself to me, and felt that I was being unfair towards him, for judging him based off of his first impression, but first impressions always last, don't they? Tee was hurt that I called him a player without even knowing him that well, he wanted to give me a chance to get to know him better, and then judge him based off of that, but I couldn't help but think to myself 'perhaps he's right, I should give him a chance, he might just prove me right'. Yes, I said right and not wrong, because my intuition was on fire then, and I had already established that I was going to get hurt by this guy, I just felt it, I just knew it, or was it self-sabotage? Was it my intuition that was speaking, or was it my trauma? But I had to be fair, give him a chance, you know? To see whether he was going to do any better, or just go on to make me regret my decision of giving him a chance. And so, I gave him the chance to prove himself to me.

A few weeks later, on a Saturday morning, I woke up to do my chores as usual. My sister had gone back home for some vac work she had applied for, so I had to clean up the place and do my laundry as well. I woke up in a pretty good mood, I made my way to the bathroom to run a bath for myself, I enjoy morning baths regardless of whether I have somewhere to go to, or not, it kind of gives me that refreshed feeling throughout the day, you know? After my bath, I decided to make some breakfast for myself, I had been trying to get back into shape because I had been off course for a while, in terms of my workouts and diet, so I made something a little healthy for myself, and that is some granola with some fresh fruit and double cream plain yoghurt. After eating, I then made my way to the bathroom to connect the washing machine, so as to commence with my chores, thank goodness the washing machine was automatic, so I wouldn't have to spend too much time doing the laundry, thus I can clean the rest of the place and probably wash the dishes as well, "dang, I'm about to kill three birds and not just two with one stone", I thought to myself, "aren't I the superwoman of all time though?".

As I was busy with my chores, my phone beeped once, and I just knew that it was a WhatsApp message, and so, I made my way up to my bed where my phone was placed, to check from whom the message was, and it was him. Tee and I had been talking for a while after our first arranged meeting, or should I say "vibing"? As that is sort of the popular word to use for people who are in the process of flirting while getting to know each other these days. Tee and I had this weird connection, we just clicked. The very first time we met, he felt like home to me, I was super comfortable and goofy around him, and that is something that rarely happens to me when I am around strangers. I always just come off as "too serious" or "too caught up with myself", which is just a mask I wear without even noticing or trying too hard. Many would say I have this "resting bitch face", and to be honest, I could never argue with that. But he was my "safe haven", okay? I could easily express how I was feeling to him, there wasn't any hint of judgement from his side. I could easily bring out my childish crazy self before him and he would join in on my madness, we had pure bliss him and I, and I truly appreciated that from him, he saw me as is, and was willing to accept me just as I was. I checked the message and Tee was asking that we meet up, at his place to be specific. I responded by letting him know that I would make my way up to his place once I was done with my chores. After about an hour, I prepped myself to go to Tee's place. I put on some tight-fitting denim, a graphic white TEE, and my white Nike Airforce sneakers, I tried to keep the outfit as simple as I could, but I just wanted to feel and look pretty when I met up with him. I then texted him to say that I was ready, and in about 3-5 minutes, he arrived, and off we drove to his place. When we arrived at Tee's place, he got out of the car to open the door for me, how adorable? I was completely flattered; I got out of the car and made my way up to him, and we both went in for a hug. We then made our way up the stairs of the block of apartments, to his place. It was a one-and-a-half-bedroom open plan apartment that had a kitchen and a bathroom as two additional rooms and an open space which could be turned into a living room or lounge(as some may call it). We made our way to the door of his apartment, and when we got inside, he tried as hard as he could to make me feel comfortable.

We were crashing on his couch, binging on some Netflix, and engaging in random conversations. Now, the whole time I could sense a bit of uneasiness from his side; he was all up in my space, I felt. Of course, I did not have an issue with him being so close to me, but it was as though he just could not hold back. At first, he kept brushing my knee as we spoke, but he never took it further, and so I didn't see any issue with that. I had told him prior to our meeting that day, that I had never had any sexual encounter with the other gender, let alone anyone, besides the fact that I was sexually assaulted and that I did not intend on doing so with anyone anytime soon, and he seemed to respect my decision. But then, on that Saturday afternoon, I would find out whether he truly respected my decision and boundaries.

He offered that I rest my upper body and head on his chest as we laid on the sofa, and I did exactly that, and to my surprise, I could feel his chest pounding like his heart was racing or fluttering. I could sense a change in the tone of his voice, it was as though he was choking on his own words, but I kind of found it cute. As we laid there together, I felt this warm yet subtle air heavily on my neck, it was his breath, I shifted my focus from that onto the screen of the flat TV screen that was seated on some TV stand. I then felt a touch of something soft yet wet on my neck, I couldn't ignore that, it was his lips. I began to feel a tingling sensation down my spine that I can't necessarily explain, but it wasn't excitement. He began to slowly, and gently kiss my neck, I could feel the passion that came with every kiss, and that frightened me. I shut my eyes, I was reminded of the encounter, the rape. Do I tell him no? Do I tell him to stop? But I wanted this with him, I had made that decision long before I made my way up to his place, although I had told him that I didn't want to, it was just to see if he would pass this test, and he didn't. So, we ended up knotting, it was hard, getting my mind to not be so caught up with what had happened to me in the past, but my mental state was clear in our experience, I guess for the first time in my life, I wanted to be in control and not feel as though I was being taken advantage of. Did you know that sex can be painful especially for victims of rape? Well, if you didn't, then now you know. It is said that individuals who have been through traumatic sexual experiences like rape, find it difficult to connect with their bodies, and it is more of a mental struggle that results in a physical struggle. When it comes to traumatic experiences like rape, one is always challenged with two choices, there's the flight and fight-mode, and if you, like me, have found yourself succumbing to rape, which is an example of the flight mode, then you are most likely to find yourself struggling to enjoy sex. The brain of a rape survivor is disconnected from the physical body. With sex, you need the two to be integrated to enjoy the full experience of sex. Getting aroused is an emotional thing, and emotions entail the physical and mental aspects of an individual, with that being said, if one's brain and body are disconnected, getting aroused will most likely be challenging for one. And that was the case with me, the penetration was just too painful, I cannot look back at that moment and describe it as pleasurable, but for the most part of it, it was okay.

After the knotting, Tee and I just cuddled up, it was cute, but I had a lot to think about. Like, I just hooked up with a guy who is in a relationship, so, I decided to confront him, about what exactly his intentions were for me, and he told me that he just wanted love from me, what an answer right? Because what is love? Was he not receiving it from his current partner, that he had to go and cuff me? I asked him if he would leave his girlfriend for me and he told me no, and said if, however, I were in a relationship with another guy, he would expect me to leave my current boyfriend. And that just turned the light switch on for me, Tee was selfish, that is one thing I learnt about him. I didn't stay any longer at his place, I got dressed and made my way to my apartment. I was annoyed, I wasn't going to settle for breadcrumbs, or be treated like an option or second choice.

But let me not play victim here, because I believe I was also villain at some point in this connection. I did this out of anger and frustration, I just wanted to poke an itsy-bitsy hole in Tee's heart, and but that was wrong of me, but at the time, although I knew it was wrong, nothing would've stopped me from going forward with my plan. It was a day after Tee and I had met up and had our souls entangled, without a shield. I don't think I would ever do this, and I wouldn't advise anyone to, safe sex is so important kids, but I got caught up in the moment that day, and just let it happen because we did not have a raincoat for that rainy day. I, I texted Tee the following day after the knotting; "Don't be mad, I should have told you sooner about this, but I was ashamed, and thought that you would be mad at me, but I am positive", and awaited his response. Tee was probably scared to death (it is so not cool to toy with someone's emotions like I did with Tee's, but he deserved it), he texted back so quickly; "are you for real?", I told him yes, and he began to ask why I wasn't on treatment, I had to lie and say I was, and honestly, had he asked me about the Meds, I would have known because I had taken Antiretrovirals for a month after my assault. I bet he was shaking, so I let him sit in the distress for a couple of minutes, but I just wasn't called for such evilness, so I had to call him and let him know that it was just a prank, I mean, that was my motive all along, to prank him, but he just wasn't buying it, I may have hurt his ego there, just a bit, and he probably didn't look at me the same after, of which I don't blame him because I was wrong for toying with his emotions like that. But one thing for sure was that Tee felt something. I have no doubt that Tee felt something for me, whether it was emotional or just physical, he felt something for me, be it love or just lust, he felt something, but he let his pride and ego get in the way, not wanting to be honest with me about his past and about his intentions for me, putting me in a third-party situation, then ghosting me, that ruined a relationship that could've turned out great, but mostly, he hurt the woman who could've loved him truly, and maybe that was all part of the lesson.

And don't get me wrong, I am in no way trying to condone cheating in relationships, that is very disgusting, but why do we always look at the women as the villains in third-party connections? I mean, I know I was wrong to engage with a man who was already connected to someone else, and I believe that if the tables were turned, I would want her to look out for me too, to say no to this man, and not be a culprit to a crime of cheating, but I guess I was still immature and lacked boundaries at the time, I knew better but just couldn't get myself to act better, and of course, I was carrying some emotional baggage from my past that clouded my judgement at the time, but that is no excuse, because at the end of the day, what happened, happened. But what about the men? Why don't they take the blame? I mean, in such instances, the man is the one who is in a commitment with this other woman, he is the one who has vowed to love her, not me, so why shouldn't he take the fall for it? Why does he get to get away with it? He clearly does not respect his partner and relationship, let alone himself, and say he maybe fell short to temptation and could not help but succumb to it, and the other woman forgives him, why can't she forgive me as well? Instead, she would rather hold onto a grudge forever, while they move on and live happily ever after. Why do women always have to be at war with one another? I understand that not all women have pure and good intentions for one another, let alone men, which is why you will find a woman who would intentionally want to cause havoc in another woman's relationship, but I cannot help but wonder where all of that stems from, is it because we were raised to believe that men are the prize? Well, that is for you to ponder on.

A few weeks after my fall out with Tee, things got cold, like negative zero degrees cold. But that was only on the internet i.e., social media. Tee became so distant that I felt as though I was forcing myself onto him, but whenever I would bump into Tee, he wanted to be all mushy and gushy with me, as if we had just woken up from the same bed, it made zero sense to me. To cut the story short, I got ghosted but my ghost still saw me as his crush, and was still very much into me, and a few weeks of me experiencing the cold winter season(silent treatment) with Tee, I saw him with his girl. Was I hurt? Of course, but I had fulfilled my assignment in his life, and him in mine, we had met for a reason, and that was for the both of us to continue to heal through our traumas, we both triggered each other, and it was such a painful experience.

For those who don't know what ghosting is, allow me to enlighten you;

Ghosting is a term used to describe a sudden cutting off of ties with someone you once had a close or personal relationship with, with no explanation or communication whatsoever. Oftentimes, people use ghosting to maintain access to you, and here's what I mean by that; because ghosting does not involve a formal cutting off of ties with someone, it leaves the door slightly opened for the individual ghosting, were they to change their mind and decide to return to the ghosted.

When I first heard about the term, I was so shocked to hear that this is a thing. Like, why can't you just be considerate enough to let someone know that you no longer have an interest in a personal relationship with them? The very same way you communicated how you had an interest in them at the beginning of your interaction, which led to the formation of your guys' relationship, why can't you follow that same route? I truly do not, and don't think I will ever be able to understand this whole concept of ghosting. And come to think of it, people find it very satisfying. Shocking! I know, right? Like how do you find pleasure in playing emotional, psychological mind games with someone, like that? Making them feel as though they are not worthy of your attention and energy by ignoring them? Especially if you guys were on speaking terms, and there was absolutely nothing bizarre that happened that may have led to such behaviour. I mean, I honestly don't care if someone is too clingy or needy, if someone said or did something hurtful to you, if you just are no longer feeling this person the way that you did before, if you have found someone else you are feeling, and are vibing with, communication with regards to the latter is so important!

When has it ever killed someone to communicate their true feelings with regards to a situation? And I know the kind of excuses running through your head at the moment; "but what if they act out on me when I communicate this to them?", "what if they take it the wrong way and in turn do something terrible to me?", "I just don't see any need to communicate this, as my lack of interest will somehow be communicated when I no longer pay them the attention or just no longer entertain them", "I just don't want to hurt their feelings", and what do you think my response to all of that is?- Immaturity! Do you think you are being cool, ghosting someone? Do you think you are saving both you and them the time and energy to explain why things have changed by just going silent and vanishing into thin air? Well, my friend, I would like to tell you otherwise, ghosting is a weakness! You are confused, aren't you? Like, how can ghosting be a sign of weakness? But unlike you, I won't leave you hanging like that with no further explanation, so let me elaborate;

Ghosting shows a weakness on your part because it exposes a lack of Maturity, like, can't you just be mature enough to let someone know that you are no longer interested in them? Instead of you childishly ignoring them and act as if they are non-existent to you, I doubt a child would even do that, so I'd like to take back my words of you being "childish" when you ghost someone and just call it immaturity. Anyways, moving right along, ghosting also exposes a lack of proper or sound communication skills from your side, you lack the skill and the confidence to head straight up to someone and communicate your change in intention, and that is why for me there is absolutely nothing cute and sexy about ghosting.

But ghosting isn't all that bad, you know? I can understand that it is a form of rejection, but perhaps pain clouds our judgment, because although he may have ghosted me for multiple other reasons, perhaps he recognised my value and worth, and him knowing that he would not live up to that, or just could not treat me the way he knew I deserved to be treated, it led him to flee out of my life, it may have been protection in disguise for the more pain I would have experienced had our connection continued. But because I was so blinded by what I hoped for between us, it made me a little bitter and angry over why he would just leave. Even so, as different as we are, some mature and some still evolving, communication remains the focal point of any relationship, and perhaps I wasn't mad about how things turned out, I wasn't mad about us not having the chance in love that I had hoped for, but rather mad about the lack of communication from his side. Lies and ghosting should and can never be used as an excuse for "wanting to protect someone", rather be honest and allow that person to brew in the truth of the matter with pain and hurt, they will recover eventually. Problem is, we try so hard to control situations most of the time, so that everything works out in our favour, but at the end of the day, that translates to selfishness. So, perhaps honesty is the best way to go about such things.

But you know what?

I love my love,

Because even with the ghosting,

I still wanted him to know so bad that my love was so gentle &
soul-soothing, I could understand if he may have felt that it was a
little intense, I don't blame him because he may have never
experienced a love as purely genuine as mine felt, but the issue
now came when I felt as though I was the only one giving to our
connection, so that's when I realized something I had never
realized about my love, that it is so demanding, demanding of
reciprocity and that is because it's too giving, demanding of one's
highest self. After all, you cannot give a love such as this from a
low vibrational frequency. My love forces you to see things
differently because you've never experienced a love such as this.
He had never experienced anything like me before, and I guess
that frightened him, to him I felt unreal, and I suppose he was not
ready for that. But I couldn't stretch myself any longer, I couldn't
suppress my energy in order to accommodate him, so I had to
leave, not because I no longer felt anything for him, not because I
hated him, yes, of course, I was disgusted and disappointed in his
actions, because how could he do me like that? How could he not
give me the princess treatment that I deserve? Unprovoked, he had
approached me and had led me to believe that he wanted forever
with me, but just a few encounters later, he switched up on me,
he left, without the decency to even let me know why, such
disrespect! I was hurt, I cried myself to sleep because I cared,
deeply for him, but I held nothing against him. I moved away
from the frequency between him and I, and I did so because he
did first. He pushed me away, and so I had to move away and never
look back. And that is because my love isn't afraid to release its

hostages from its bondage, to allow them the freedom of exploration till they find their heart's true desires.

I cannot say it was easy though, letting go. I can't say I didn't care any longer, but I needed to do it, to do it for me. A love such as mine needs protection, because were it to ever fall into the wrong hands, it would be entirely contaminated with what's called "sabotage energy", an energy that focuses too much on the past negatives that it loses its focus so much so, that it no longer can see the good in everything it experiences from the now, to the future, and I never wanted to be influenced to stop loving and giving from the purest and deepest roots of my heart, as a result of my past hurts and pain, because that's what I would later on attract, and that was never what I craved. What I crave instead is;

A love so gentle that it soothes my soul from the fear of heartache. I desire a love that is understanding, understanding of my insecurities that have been tied to me from childhood, A love that is willing to get into the container of my brain and unravel my thoughts, as messy as they are. A love so genuine I don't get anxiety whenever it isn't validated. I pray for a love that sees my scars from past hurts, and without judging, understands that I'm relearning certain things about myself, and so it chooses to allow me time and space to heal, without being pushy. I seek a love that is not only attracted to my seductive eyes, nor just the physicality of this Feminal Being, but a love that is drawn to my kindness, to my compassion, to the way I feel deeply and express myself so, a love invested in my intellect and my perspective of the world.

So, what is my ideal love, you ask?

Well, tell you what, for me;

Love is not meant to be a minefield where you have to tread carefully. Yes, it's risky, but Love should be reckless but not so negligent, it should be superintended. Love should not be a battlefield that leaves one wrecked or drained like they are from war, Love, like the river, should be a stream of souls that flow effortlessly into one another, merging into one. Love is reciprocity, in energy and time, forget unrequited love. Love is risky, you bet all your cards onto the table aware of the fact that it might not work out, but still bidding for a positive outcome. Love is pure, Love is not ruled by a sense of self, it's a compromise. Love for me is not about temporary pleasures, it is forever or never at all. Love is not surface levelled, Love uncovers every hidden aspect below the surface, Love is simple, yet complex. It is like a labyrinth of emotions that will have you drowning in the ocean of fear and uncertainty, but in the end; love chooses, it chooses what it truly wants, and it sticks with it. Love is what you make it to be, Love breaks the rules, it is not bound by protocol, Love is nothing you have ever imagined, Love erases every idea you've ever had of it, it is a feeling of renewal, a feeling of Familiarity, a sense of home that is. My idea of love does not even exist, because Love, Love is a mystery waiting to be unfolded.

And that is why I dedicate this letter,

To the girl who, like me, is such a sucker for love;

[**Song of Solomon 3: 5**]

I,
Pray you learn to fall in love with yourself first,
Pray you fall in love with every inch of your body, scars, and all your flaws – all!
Pray you learn to embrace every insecurity that drowns your mind,
Pray you learn to make God your first love,
Pray you allow God to be your validator before anyone else!
Pray you know you're worthy and deserving of love,
Pray you know how you should be treated because you are a Princess, part of Royalty and you carry royal breath in you,
Pray you get to know who you are before you step out into a relationship,
Pray you discover your true purpose here on this earth,
Pray that God gives you the Spirit of Discernment, to know the difference between what's truly yours and what's counterfeited,
Pray that you be gentle with every part of you that's been broken, bruised, and hurt and that you allow yourself time to heal before you give a part of yourself to someone else,
Pray you're comfortable with being alone before you get with someone else,
Pray you first become WHOLE before finding the "love of your life",

Pray you don't give bits and pieces of who you are to just any, and everyone who's undeserving!

And lastly, I Pray that when you're finally ready to give & receive love, the man you will be in love with has godly intentions.

Letter from Ms Rendy

CHAPTER 12- CHANGING THE NARRATIVE

Nativity.

The process of the making is such a sensual escapade. Regardless of whether it is at two in the morning, three in the afternoon, or in the late evenings, planned or unplanned, there is never really a right time for such matters because when nature calls and consent is present, there's just a magic that explodes when two genetics form to create one unique combination of a Being. Conceiving is a whole different process on its own. From the very fine detail of one's fingerprints, to the precision that goes into one's anatomy, life creation is just beautiful. But giving birth must be scary, I mean, that would explain why all babies squall the minute they exit their first place of residence, but birth can be such a painful, yet beautiful experience to go through.

Nevertheless, the beginning of birthing life is in copulation, and that would be the best place to start, therefore, allow me to touch on this hot topic of sex.

I am literally cringing right now, the sound of that is just, should I say, too shameful? But you know what? We're going to talk about sex, well, I'm going to write about sex, and you are going to read about it. So, where do I begin?

Sex. Such a beautiful act of love and affection designed as a form of intimacy by a Creator who is very intimate himself. Sex is an act of merging two souls together, connecting them into one unit. Sex is bonding. It is a contract, a soul contract to stick together beyond the physical. Sex is not just a physical act, yes, it involves the physical parts of the body and cooperation from those parts to function together to get the job done, but more than anything, sex is spiritual. Sex is a ritual, a ritual between two people and their Creator, creating a knot, a knot which is an agreement to become unified. Sex is a safe space for vulnerability. Sex is, "I open up myself to you – raw, and you do the same". It Is; "look into my soul and I'll look into yours, allow me to give you a glimpse of who I truly am beneath this shell". Sex is an exchange, that "let us share parts of each other with one another". Sex is opening a portal into each other's worlds, to move about between the two worlds, and to grasp what you can from both worlds.

But, in the world that we live in today? What I have just said about sex is all a fairy tale for some because sex is something totally contradictory to what I have just mentioned above. Sex has become a form of entertainment, that sacred moment between two partners, has become a show for the world to see. It has become a group assignment, as it is now between multiple partners. Sex has become a business deal, that; "how much do you charge for a few hours of your body to myself?" Sex is like the banking system these days, that "Tap-N-Go". Sex is wild. Sex has lost its essence, its initial purpose of reproduction. I know sex isn't just about making babies, sex is meant to be pleasurable, an act between two souls submerging into the depths of one another. And although sex these days, isn't as bashed, although it is behaviour that is becoming more acceptable, not only between married couples, but the unmarried too, between young teenage boys and girls, and between married/committed men or women and their sides, that will never take away from the fact that sex has just become pervy, it's really really nasty, hence most people are still too ashamed to even talk about it without cringing.

Growing up, I have always known sex to be an act between older persons, spouses to be specific. Remember how your parents used to lie to you when you were a kid, about how you were conceived? If not, then you must have had a boring childhood, *jokes*. They would make up stories about how they found you at the hospital or how a huge bird dropped you off at their doorstep, or just something silly like that, and that was because sex wasn't just some conversation you could throw out there, it was dignified and you just couldn't talk about sex to just anybody, your kids especially. And of course, you teach your kids about these things at a certain age, but can we just pause for a moment while I give you a depiction of something you need to use your imagination creatively and turn into a masterpiece of art? Imagine seeing a young girl, 12 years of age, how do you tell that she's 12 years? Well, she has not yet started her high school and you can tell that by the school rain jacket she's wearing covering the watermelon she has just had for lunch, written "Year 7, 2021" with the name of the school. She's pregnant, at 12years of age, in primary school. And you can't help but think to yourself, how did she get pregnant? Like, did she actually have sexual intercourse with a boy? Like, how? And I know that back in the day, in the early centuries, it was normal for girls at the age of twelve to fall pregnant, and that was because the family maybe wasn't so well off thus the female child was traded for marriage to a boy or even an older man who was well off, in fact, in some African countries, this is still a thing. Another reason for early childhood pregnancies was because girls were taught that marriage was the end goal, they were moulded and prepared for marriage from a very early stage, and you know what? I love and respect marriage, I believe too that sex was meant for marriage, but see, the moral of the story here is

"Knowledge can be good and informing, yet so damaging when it is given to the right individual at the wrong time".

Although there isn't a right age for a girl to get her period, most young girls start their period as early as nine to twelve years old. Getting one's period is a sign that the female body is ready for reproduction, ready to produce another human, and if one does not fall pregnant during their "cycle"(a word used to describe the process of preparation of a woman's body to create life), then vaginal bleeding will occur as the tissue lining that was created by the uterus, as a result of preparation for pregnancy is shed, the egg(ova) that was not useful and blood, is released from the female's body. But just because one's body is ready for reproduction; it doesn't necessarily mean that one is ready to bring another human onto this earth and parent them.

I guess sex is not as beautiful as I thought it to be, well at least not in this world. And the truth is it is all our fault. We have allowed this perverted version of sex to exist among us for way too long now and have adopted it as our norm. As a community that is "open to a lot of things", I believe we have messed up right there because truly speaking, I do not know if we could ever be able to restore the true meaning of what sex is. I mean, not to say that it cannot be done, the restoration of sex's beauty, or that the damage cannot be undone, but so as to say that it's going to take a lot of unlearning and relearning for a lot of us. I wonder if more and more sexual assault cases like rape, are increasingly high because people find it to be okay to have sex with someone they are physically attracted to because "that is a way of showing affection", because "if you like someone, you have to sleep with them, as 'sex is love making', we are making love". Sex has been downplayed to a point where it is no longer that deep, "it's just sex, nothing more", but really now, is it?

You are probably waiting for me to talk about soul ties, aren't you? And you know what? I know it is very cliché and typical of me to talk about soul ties under the topic of sex, but I'm doing it anyway, and my reason for that being, me not talking about soul ties under this hot topic of sex would result in me not having done justice to this topic, so, without wasting any more time, let me talk about knots, right about now;

Soul ties, what are these? I know for one I have always just assumed that soul ties were something that only related to people who were sleeping around, people who were being physical, having sex, especially those who were doing it out of wedlock, but as I grew older, as I researched more on it, I started to learn so much more than I knew when I first heard about soul ties. So, before I lose you, I'm going to delve right into this topic.

First thing's first, let's look at what the soul entails:
The soul, from what I understand, is everything that has to do with your emotions, thoughts & feelings, so, that would mean that when we refer to soul ties, what we mean is that two souls have been entangled, that one was once or is currently invested emotionally in a relationship with someone, and now when that relationship comes to an end, they can't entirely move on, so they try to move on but they still feel somehow bound to that particular individual as a result of the knot that has been created, causing them to remain tied to the other soul, and that is all because of the

emotions they may have invested so much into that particular relationship. Soul ties are a form of emotional attachment. Having spent a couple of days, weeks, or months getting to know someone, spending a lot of time together, and daydreaming about someone, you create this attachment to that particular person. The only reason why sex is considered the biggest element of soul ties is that the act alone is a fluctuation, or for the sake of a better word, "see-saw" of emotions, it involves vulnerability, and vulnerability is invasion, invasion into one's inner shadow that not everyone gets to see, and I mean, being vulnerable isn't something that everyone can easily give into, sex is almost like submission, submission from your conscious self, to your subconscious self. And now, after having said that, I realize that friendships can form soul ties, crushes can form soul ties, sex too but it's not only limited to those connections that I have just mentioned, however, for the sake of keeping things short and sweet, I will only touch on those three. Allow me to elaborate, will you?

So, when you begin a friendship with someone, I mean it's a serious relationship, okay? You will feel tied to this person because maybe you guys spend so much time together, you share so much of yourselves with each other, and there's just so much investing happening there, hence, when so many friendships come to an end, you feel as though a part of you has gone missing, because the Knot detangles a little but not entirely, when the distance is formed. Moving along to crushes, "oh, that boy is cute", or "damn, I met this girl and baby girl is fineee", so, you find out a bit more about them, their name, where they stay, if they have social media, if so, then on which platform just so you can start stalking them?

And you do, and boy you're head over heels over this individual, you can't stop thinking about them, you master the confidence to follow them and slide right into their DMs, you are trying your luck, okay!? And there's absolutely nothing wrong with that. You guys begin to talk and whatever, but you realize that they aren't actually that interested, I mean, yes, they are friendly towards you and whatever, but not in a way they would, you know "like to take it further". So, you stop talking as you have been initially, and you begin to realize that they are now seeing somebody else, you become a little pissed and envious, because "what do they have that I don't?" And now, you've got to let go of your crush on them, but you liked that girl, you liked that boy, you still have a little hope that maybe, just maybe things might work out between the two of you, but what you don't realize is that you are tightening the Knot onto this rope, and the longer you hold onto this person and this relationship that "almost" happened, the stronger the tie gets.

But any who, let us get to the juicy part, let's talk about sex, hope you're not cringing right now. I know how most of us feel about this sacred act. I always find it awkward when sex scenes come up on the television and I'm sitting with a parent, like should I look away? Should I change the channel as I'm the one holding the remote control? Should I just start a conversation with my parent to at least distract both of our focus from the television, and ultimately the scene? Yes, sex is awkward, I feel super awkward right now just writing about it. But what I have learned for married couples is that sex is beautiful, sex was created by God, to be nice, and good, and you know, fun and amazing! But our generation has damaged God's concept of sex. And I get that not all married couples enjoy their marriages, especially not in this day and age where infidelity and cheating is the theme for most marriages or relationships, but I believe the reason why most religions or cultures preferred that sex take place between couples that were married, was because they understood the spiritual depth of it, that it wasn't just some game between two people, where one object goes in and out of the other, it is a ritual, a spiritual act. And so, imagine merging with different kinds of individuals, taking on their energies and vibrations? Not cool, bro! What am I yielding to? I believe we are Spiritual Beings, and not to sound like a pastor on a pulpit or some spiritual guide, but if we were to yield to the concept of energy, the inhalations(oxygen) and exhalations(carbon dioxide) we breathe in and out of our lungs, are air, and when we talk about air, air is energy, energy in this case is the vibrations of air, it would therefore be safe to say that our bodies consist of energy. But like I said before, I am no scientist, neither am I learned in that field, but take it like this; Science says "energy is one's ability to do work", therefore whatever movement or action your body creates, it is as a result of the vibrations within your air(breathe), together with other molecules in your body, for example, when you speak, the sound you produce is transmitted by vibrations in the air("your breath", together with your vocal cords i.e., muscle bands and tissues in your voice box, vibrate together to create the sound of your voice), so when you breathe in and out(that is what we are constantly doing, even though we may not realize it), when you speak, and whatever other thing that human beings do, you are constantly vibrating energy throughout your body, therefore sex could also be seen as a transmission of energy, an exchange of vibrations between two persons. And although I have just explained energy in a scientific way, try to picture it in a spiritual way, rumours have it that God, depending on what or who you believe in, breathed life into us, His breath, which is basically that air/ energy that I have just referred to above, and because God is not a human being but a spiritual Being, that means that the breath we carry in our lungs is spiritual energy and we thus need to realize that it is sacred, thus having sex i.e., merging our energies with that of others, can be dangerous when you do not know how contaminated their energies are. But also, because sex is about reproduction, and because humans were made to connect, think of the many individuals we bring to life, who feel disconnected, and not to say that children born into relationships that end up being broken(because of separated parents), do not end up doing just fine without both their parents being connected, but sometimes that gap does exist, where you find one questioning why they do not have both parents, "why is my dad happily married to another woman with kids, and not my mother and I? Maybe they just don't love me enough", which is of course not always the case, but a reality that can exist in a child's mind who grows up to be an adult. And even though sex doesn't always lead to the creation of mankind(as there are a lot of ways to prevent life these days, and also ways used as a measure of safety but resulting in prevention), sex creates an emotional attachment, as explained already, and although detaching physically from the other individual can be easy, the emotional detachment can be painful once such a strong emotional bond has been created.

For most people, sex is nasty, it's disgusting - the way they present it. The pornography on the Internet is all just too much to bear witness to. God's purpose has always been that sex would be an agreement between two people, a binding agreement to be specific. That they were joining into one, and that's why it's seen as a married couple's act because marriage represents a life-long commitment to one partner, it is unity. "Sex is a covenant, going to the government and telling them that you want to be with this person forever and ever Amen, isn't the only actual agreement in God's eyes, throwing some wedding and inviting people to witness as you say I do isn't the actual agreement, the agreement happens when the hammer strikes the nail - that's the actual covenant". So, yes! If you thought soul ties entail sex, you weren't entirely wrong at all, because sex involves emotions (emotions are physical and can be measured by blood flow and brain activity), as well as feelings (feelings are mental and can't be precisely measured).

But wait, don't get me wrong, it's not that I'm saying that the 'holy matrimony' isn't important, in fact, I am saying the exact opposite of that. Holy matrimonies are for witness's purposes, remember, a wedding and a marriage are two different things but very much interdependent, don't you ever forget that. For a wedding to exist, two people must have come to an agreement to get into a marital union with one another, and for a marriage to begin, they must have taken that step, to involve witnesses to come experience and be present as they take this step forward in their relationship. Yes, you heard that right, weddings aren't just for entertainment purposes, it is for your family, friends, and God to bear witness to

186

this beautiful act of love and step you are taking in your relationship with your partner, to merge two beautiful souls on their own, into an even more beautiful soul connection, a soul union. So, yes, of course, weddings these days are a bit over the top and seem to only be for entertainment purposes, but if you have the money then, why not? Marriage on the other hand is the long term commitment, that "I'm sticking around to do this life thing with you", marriage is growth, that "I'm here and I will be there to witness you as you shed some of your old skin, as you burst out of your cocoon to become the beautiful and free spirited YOU, you've always been building up to be. As you immerge out of the ground and sprout into the fruitful plant you were always sown to be, I will help you through all of that, as you too will bear witness to my own growth", but most importantly marriage is a choice, that "I'm choosing to love you, and commit to you and only you because I want you to be that soul partner that I experience the next couple of days of my existence on the face of the earth with, I want to be the one to root for you as you continue to fulfil your life's purpose, and a more obvious yet blessed reason would be, I want to start my own little family with you, have a part of my genetics and your DNA come together to form little versions of ourselves, and have those little versions call you daddy or mommy because you're the one person I see myself creating a killer combo of a life with".

Going back to the topic of soul ties, it is clear to see that soul ties aren't just limited to sex. I can feel someone already boiling, I apologise if I've stepped on your little toes, but I felt the need to share. But don't be scared, don't be afraid to love hard, do not stop caring for people, this for me, was just an informational piece to you, because you know what "they" say; sharing is caring. So, continue to make connections with people but stay alert, some people are just temporary, but are there to play some part in your life even though it is short-lived, therefore, if you do feel that you have already invested so much of yourself in certain individual's lives unnecessarily, pray about it and actively work towards untangling the strings that bind you to people who no longer serve a purpose in your life, besides, God is in the business of breaking those chains binding you and slowing you down from exercising your true potential and fulfilling your purpose!

In fact, let us pray right now;
> *Dear Lord,*

> *Thank you for being a Healer. Today, I present all that I am before you and ask that you unwind me from any bondages that I may have gotten myself tied up in, after having entangled myself in connections with certain individuals. I ask that You set me free, I ask for discernment and pray that You will grant me control over my emotions and feelings, and desires. Heal my soul, renew my thoughts, and make me whole again. I receive your healing.*

> *In Jesus' name, Amen!*

With more on the topic of sex, sex begins with a relationship, once a relationship has been established (well, in this world it can be platonic, dating, marriage, or just the acquaintances kind of relationship), then can we tap into this activity of mating. Sex is an adventure, that "I'll dig deep into your soul and explore parts of you that no one else ever has". Sex is a mystery, you don't know how it's going to happen, will it be pleasurable, or will it just be okay? Will you feel connected to this other person on a higher level? However, it would be wrong to say that sex is just a measure of compatibility because sex alone does not make a relationship work. Not to discourage anyone by sounding like I am trying to say that relationships are a handyman's work, but relationships are investments, and just like investments, it is all about risks and rewards. "The higher the risk, the higher the return and the lower the risk, the lower the return." So, depending on how many eggs you put into your basket, that will be the reflection of your return; if you put in a bit of communication, and a dash of vulnerability, it could work, and let's not forget to add a lot of loyalty, but remember; not all investments are worth it, you can only continue to invest in something in which you see a return and if not, then maybe you need to reconsider that investment, and not to say that in every season your tree will bear fruit even though you keep watering it, and that is because sometimes it just isn't the right season for that tree to blossom. But then what do you do? You keep watering the tree, you prune it, you cut off some old branches and even learn new useful tricks or tactics for the growth of your plant in that particular season, and in due time, in the right season, you watch that tree i.e., relationship bloom and produce fruits. And but of course, this doesn't come easy, like who wants to touch cold water during the winter season just because they are trying to nurture some plant that isn't even going to produce any fruit until the summer? But just keep one thing in mind; "great things don't come easy", not to say that we have to suffer for all good things in our lives, but everything has a level of difficulty or challenge that it poses, you just have to be wise enough to choose the ones worthwhile. But then again, what about those trees that are just nasty weeds? What do we do with those? I mean weeds can look pretty too, okay? They can be useful, for instance in herbal treatment, or for that high we need for some emotional release, but these aren't plants we constantly need, they don't necessarily bear fruits, unlike fruit-bearing trees which provide us with the everyday nutrients we need to survive, same goes with certain relationships, they may seem useful at first, because of the entertainment they provide, but aren't necessarily sustainable for the long-term, and at some point may be emotionally taxing, and you are going to have to decide if they are worth investing in or not. Nonetheless, sometimes your outcome will be favourable and other times it will feel like a waste of time, energy, and effort, which might lead to a lot of individuals rather sticking to the lazy kind of love which requires little to no effort but also does not necessarily lead anywhere, but in all aspects, it all boils down to the question of:

"Is love alone enough in a relationship?"

Like most of you, my answer used to be no, but it wasn't until I could fully understand the concept of love that my answer switched to yes, because what is love? Love is more than just a feeling; it is more than just the butterflies that you feel rising to the surface of your stomach whenever you see or think of your partner or crush. "Love is both a noun and a verb", cliché, right? But here is what I mean:

Love, a noun, a feeling of 'I know you only because you feel familiar and I feel safe around you, a feeling of I want to be with you and spend the rest of my eternity protecting you', but Love as a verb is all the work required to make it work in a relationship, you cannot stick around someone's life when they are faced with challenges unless if you love them of course. Love is a doing word, you love someone because of the feelings you feel for them, but you choosing to stick around during and through the hard times? That too is love, because love is being there for someone no matter what, love is compromise, a modus vivendi reached by two totally different individuals, to give to one another and continue to grow and coexist with one another. Love is selfless, that "I'm willing to put you first or to put your needs above mine, not because I don't love myself or care about myself enough, but because I, myself am enough and my jug is more than enough to fill two cups". Love is compassionate, that; "You messed up, but I understand that you are not perfect and that you are learning as you go, so I show compassion instead of judging you". Love is showing patience, that "I know you've been hurt before, broken and bruised, I know you feel a little lost but I'm willing to hold your hand as you journey through your healing process, without rushing you". Love is sacrifice, giving not because I'm obliged to but because I'm willing to go the extra mile just for you. If you see love as only a feeling then you're going to struggle with keeping any relationship going because the work element of love is just too much effort, but if you see love as both a feeling and an act then you are set, Because "I'm doing this for my partner, family, friend, or stranger as an act of love, and not because I'm obligated to do so, I don't have to do it just because I say I love them, or just to show that I do, but because of the love I have inside of me, it's just natural for me to do so and so is it for them".

Uncomfortable growth.

There are most phases in life that force you to break out of your shell. Of course, we are all meant to evolve but there's that constant fear of where life will take us, which makes growing feel so uncomfortable, but the only reason why growth can be uncomfortable is that we don't feel ready enough or prepared for it - the changes, the losses, and the uncertainty of succeeding at this life thing, the thought of it all gives one a tingling sensation down their spinal column. But one unarguably honest fact about growth is that, like death, it is inevitable, we all must grow. And here's the proof;

Just a few years back, you were learning to crawl and get on your own two little feet, you were learning to say your first few words, let alone write your name, those were your tough times. But now, as you grow a little older, you have so much at hand, you have big life decisions to make, from career choices, to choosing who you want to spend the rest of your life with, to changing nappies and choosing which school is best for the kids, and saving up money for retirement, now, that is growth, and it is unavoidable. I bet we could all agree that being a kid is one of the easiest tasks this life has to offer, you are stress-free, without a care in the world and then, all of a sudden you are going through puberty - changes, and it all feels a little too weird for you, but you come to terms with it, the fact that this is nature at its course and so, you breathe a little, learn to embrace the changes of your physique, amongst others but just as you're getting comfy, life throws you with another shebang, you're choosing which career field you want to end up in, I mean for some, this process is such a breeze, whereas many of us struggle with choosing what we'd like to do for the rest of our lives, and well at that point you're stressed out because honestly, you're thinking to yourself "well, aren't I useless? Not knowing what I have to do with my life has got to be the most disgraceful thing ever", and at that stage honestly, you're allowed to feel exactly that way because your feelings are always valid, but you can never allow them to dictate how the rest of your life will turn out, because, it's now a few years down the line, you are going with whatever career choice you have picked, or even better, it looks like you are getting the hang of it - this life thing, and that's because you are maybe doing something a little different from what your choice initially was a few years ago, and you seem to be enjoying it, right? Right. And just as you are in the process of minding your business, you meet this other gender, you start talking, and oh my, the butterflies filling up your stomach!? Beautiful! You can't help but act stupid around them, well, isn't that cute? Things get a little serious, or should I say, "very serious", they are all you're thinking of, your future plans involve them and theirs you, you are deciding on what you're going to name your babies, how adorable! You have a few disagreements here and there, but it's nothing that can't be fixed. Oh, wait a minute, you thought this was going to be that love story with a cute ending, didn't you? Oops! I'm sorry to be such a bore, because after four long years of commitment with this person, you both come to an understanding that things are different, you both want different things, and there's absolutely nothing wrong with that or even worse, they cheat and mess up, what a disappointment! At first, it's a little hard to come into terms with, the fact that things didn't work out, but you get the hang of it and you move on, you're doing okay now, better than you were before and things are looking up for you, or like some of us you are drowning on the side of the ocean while the relationship experts are having the time of their lives on a 16ft yacht, but don't be envious, you can't lose hope, you will meet your Prince charming or Cinderella, your forever partner! Your past relations have shaped your character, you are wiser and there's so much more you are aware of now, that you had no clue of before. You have learned certain things from your connections, and you are letting go of certain beliefs that you once held about relationships, about yourself too. And remember; there's so much to this life thing than just finding a partner, you have your whole future staring right at you for you to be so consumed by romantic relationships because you know what? "Romantic love is not everyone's need, it's not even a requirement in the Bible, it's a choice and not everyone will desire it". Our generation is so obsessed with being in a relationship, finding a partner and everyone just feels incomplete without a romantic kind of love in their lives, it's sad really, how people invest so much into meaningless relationships all because they do not want to end up alone one day. Personally? I'm okay with being alone. I would rather be alone than to build with an individual who is full of deceit, betrayal and probably doesn't even want me or is just using me. I would rather die alone from a natural cause of death than stick around with another individual in a relationship that will one day be the death of me. When I say, "I don't need a man and that I just want him", I mean it from the bottom of my heart. I don't say it from a place of hurt or pain, but I say it because I don't need a man to fulfil me, I am very much capable of fulfilling my own desires and dreams without any man beside me, I have the capability to be all that I have been called to be without romance being involved in my life, but I would be lying to myself if I were to say that I don't want it because I do want it, I do desire it, but I could do without it. See, the difference between needing a romantic love and wanting it, is that not having romantic love in my life will in no way hinder me from fully growing and becoming the woman that I have been designed to be, but having it would also be a great thing, an enhancement in my life, because I get to fulfil also my "other" humanly desires that are led sometimes by temptation and just human nature, with someone who also wants to fulfil theirs. It would also mean that I get to build and grow with an accountable partner beside me and that's beautiful, but as I said already; I can fulfil whatever purpose I have been tasked with, with or without romantic love being present.

And I mean, I get it, as humans, we have this void so deep that we need filled, we were made to connect and so we long for intimacy, we long to be felt, not just physically but elsewhere, it's a longing that we have that another human could never fully fulfil for us but could try. We long to be seen, to be understood and not only heard, we seek hearts that are accepting of all of our faults and without judgement; help us fall in love with our very own flaws, we just want to feel safe in our vulnerability, in the hands of someone or something. And that is why we find ourselves having casual sex or "hook-ups", because we long to feel and to be felt, even if it is just for a short while. We find ourselves coming out of one relationship and going into the next because we long for something, for someone who will finally get us, with whom we will just click, but when we meet other individuals whom we have differences with, or who highlight certain parts of ourselves which we are too scared to deal with, we flee, hoping the other side will have greener pastures for us, and when we do not find that there; we run again, but perhaps it's time we take a look at ourselves and have honest conversations with our inner man like, what is it that you seek? What is it that you long for? – self-introspection, instead of looking outside ourselves for something only we can offer ourselves, then maybe relationships wouldn't be so draining, we wouldn't be so needy to our partners, we wouldn't seek saviours or projects in our relationships, but lovers.

But also, when I say I don't need a man, what I truly mean is that I don't need a man who is going to abuse and use my love. I don't need a man who's going to breadcrumb me because he's busy juggling me with multiple other women, I don't need a man who doesn't respect me only because I'm a woman and he's a man, plus has little concern for me because if he did, then he would never put me in a position where I feel disrespected by him. I don't need one who isn't sure about me but won't let go because he's afraid that if he does, he will have lost out on a good woman once he finally makes up his mind on what he truly wants and realizes what a gem I am. I don't need a liar who's going to manipulate me and sweet talk me into thinking that he wants me when in actual fact he doesn't but just likes the attention and ego boost that I give to him. I don't need a man who's not going to step up to the table and meet me where I'm at because "well, I'm a man and you're a woman and I don't need a woman to tell me what to do or how to do it", all because of his insecurities and fears of me being a threat to his masculinity so, he'd rather I, dim my light to make him feel good about himself than deal with his insecurities and recognise how blessed he is to have been connected with a strong force like myself, no!

What I do need, is a man who understands that we are equals, him and I, and that there isn't anyone superior to the other. I need a man who is going to respect me and actively show that, by not putting me in positions or situations that make me appear as worthless and/or undervalued. I'm going to need this man to realize that it's not just about the money, and of course, I understand that men's "default purpose" is that of provision, but I don't need provision only in monetary terms, sure I crave financial stability and men do too, but I mean financial independence has been on the horizon for both men and women so, what I need instead is to feel protected and loved, I need to not only be told that I'm respected and valued but I need to be shown that too, and my reason for being so demanding? It's because I know what I bring to the table; I am not just going to bring a pretty face and a fat ass(although some men are pretty much attracted to that), I bring stability, baby! Emotional stability, spiritual stability, financial stability, with a little bit of entertainment, of course, you name it child! Truth is some men are threatened by women who are whole on their own because they fear the responsibility of them having to step up and fully operate in their wholeness, as their highest selves. They feel challenged, so they would rather settle for mediocre love because that means less responsibility. Not to disgrace a woman who has a pretty face and has been beautifully bodily structured, because that doesn't mean that such women lack the emotional intelligence and maturity but referring to "immature little girls trapped in a woman's body "- because in as much as there are immature men who lack direction, there are women who are that way too. And fortunately, most of these women have been blessed with pretty faces and great behinds, who have nothing more to offer than just that, and they very well use those to their advantage, to get men wrapped around their fingers, and men surely do fall for that, hence, the reason why I'm referring to pretty faces and big behinds. But in all honestly, assuming that we were being realistic, how is a pretty face and a great behind going to help us in a relationship when we are faced with financial difficulty in our partnership? Hmm? Unless of course, we decide to go into the business of "selling", *jokes*. But are we going to fuck our problems away, or as a man are you not going to need a woman who can think, work, and pray her way out of difficulties? Well, those are just some of the financial and spiritual aspects of stability that I, and many other women bring to the table, and, with the emotional stability that I bring, I will love you the way that you need to be loved, I will be there when you feel as though you are on a sinking ship and no one fully comprehends you or what you are going through. I'll hold your hand; remind you of how strong you are and all that you are capable of, I will be there to ground you; when that emotional storm begins to surface up and you feel as though you have nothing or nobody to anchor you, I'll be there not only for the good times but for the bad too, because as much as men don't like to admit it?

They just want to be loved up on, to not only be heard but understood, they crave the attention and reassurance that remind them that they too matter, and that they are worthy of a love so deep that isn't so hard on them but gentle and a little rough around the edges. Men love to feel and think that they are in control, hence, they crave a submissive partner, but how do I submit to a man who does not respect me, a man who does not care for me? And so, when you often hear a woman scream from the top of her lungs; "I don't need no man, cos baby I've got me", she's just tired; tired of giving so much to someone who expects a lot from her but isn't willing to offer the same, so all she ends up thinking is "well, if I can give so much to someone else, then surely I can give the same to myself". And it isn't that she lacks trust or that she just cannot submit, no, in fact, she is very much capable of trusting and being submissive, it is the fear; fear of knowing the pain of being so vulnerable and completely giving to someone else, only for them to use and abuse your vulnerability towards them to their advantage, and then having them leave as if you never meant a thing to them. The sad truth is that this woman can love deeply, and trust completely, but she is just scared of opening up again, only to be hurt.

And yes, I know what you're thinking "what does this not-experienced enough year old know?", and I can totally understand where you are coming from, because I too still have a long way to go on this life journey, and my opinions from today will most probably vary from my opinions a decade-plus years later, that's if any of us will still be around. But my conclusion right now, at this point in my life is that; as much as growth is uncomfortable, it's necessary. Growth isn't an age thing, it does not happen every year when you turn the page on the calendar and it's your birth month and day; it is a choice, a conscious decision one makes; to search within themselves and declutter what no longer serves them, to learn to embrace the challenges they are presented with and take a lesson or two from those, to continuously adapt through all the changes, and so, no one can ever say that they have mastered the way of life, therefore, one thing we all have in common in this life is that; we are constantly evolving, in our relationships, careers, and selves, but we all learn to adapt to these constant changes we're faced with; as we learn, we hold on to some of our past acquired bits of knowledge and information from our experiences or observations, but we also unlearn certain behaviours, and that is all part of growing up.

Unlearning.

We all have our different values and morals, our own "truths" that have been deeply ingrained in us from birth and of which we have kind of just carried throughout our life's journey because "that's our normal", but the issue with values is that they tend to make us associate ourselves with ignorance. Because you believe so much in how things should be in a particular way, or because there is some set of rules that have been ingrained deeply into your soul, you get veiled on just your opinion and facts alone, and you aren't as open minded to the world and the changes presented to you.

But as I continue to evolve and become aware of the different aspects of life and obtain more and more knowledge, I cannot continue to associate myself with Ignorance.

Truth is; we all do reach a stage in life where what we once lived by, what we thought was once right at one point of our life is no longer applicable to who we now are. See, there are levels to this thing called life, and I can understand if your family recipe has been working for you all these years, but you most definitely cannot use the same recipe that was used by your great-great-great-grandparents without adding a twist to it because the truth is; how things were back in the day are not as they are right now, maybe similar but not the same. Your path is different, maybe similar to someone else's but absolutely not a duplicate, you can draw inspiration from someone else's recipe, but at some point, you are going to have to create your very own life, and live it, and that means having to unlearn certain ideas that you had about yourself that were maybe influenced by people's opinions, your family included!?

I am a firm believer and follower of Christ, I'm strict on what the Bible says but that does not mean that I do not fumble on a daily. I used to be so hard on myself whenever I sinned, or should I say "made a mistake?", I would beat myself up because even though I knew better, I still chose not to do better, but in my belief, I have reached a point where I'm more compassionate towards myself when I make a "mistake" because I am not perfect and I will never be perfect, but I try and that is okay, that is enough, and that has been part of my journey of unlearning. Now, having reached that point, I now know that I will never force my beliefs or opinions onto anyone else because what I truly and genuinely believe is that we are all called to walk on this path of self-discovery. My views might just change at any point in time as I continue to learn and evolve but that doesn't mean that I cannot hold onto what I believe in at whatever point in time I'm at; when my mind's container (i.e., the brain) is only limited to, or has only acquired a certain amount of information, but that also does not mean that I should be ignorant to everything else, facts or opinions, around me.

Ignorance, Ignorance is associated with being unenlightened, so, looking at ignorance in that sense, being ignorant simply means that one is unaware, uneducated, lacks the information or knowledge necessary to tackle a particular situation, that would be the basic definition of what ignorance is, which describes ignorance in the best way possible, but I beg to differ, not because I don't entirely agree with the definition that our good friend "Google" has provided us with, but because that is not always the case with ignorance, ignorance from my very own perspective is;

sometimes being very much woke i.e. aware and informed, but choosing to stick with your own beliefs and ideas, instead of choosing to be teachable, accepting that you're not always going to be right, and being compassionate over those around you with different ideas, views, and beliefs to yours.

We all reach a point in time where what we once thought was best for us, no longer seems to be, but without self-judgement and harshness towards ourselves, what we can do moving along is to gently accept that the decisions and choices we have made in the past were best for the version we were then, so, there's no need to be mad and/or feel stupid, but instead a need exists for us to take on the lessons, create boundaries for ourselves, establish change and make decisions for the person we are now and will be in the future.

CHAPTER 13- THE AFTERMATH

"The effects of rape are not only physical nor just psychological; they are both psychological and/or physical traumas that the victim has to deal with for the rest of their life."

This part of the chapter will be based on the following topics: PTSD, Globus pharyngis, the risk of pregnancy, STDs, STIs and HIV/AIDS, different degrees of depression, and anxiety disorder.

The first medical condition I will speak on will be Globus pharyngis, Globus pharyngis is a sensation or feeling that something is stuck in one's throat, or that there is a lump blocking one's throat. This is more of an emotional state of being but can be deemed to also be a physical issue, which I'll explain further down below to give you a more realistic explanation, but it is mainly caused by sudden stress, being or feeling too anxious, or having an actual object stuck in one's throat.

The second condition will have to be PTSD. PTSD is short for post-traumatic stress disorder; it is the most common symptom that most doctors diagnose victims of trauma with. So, what kind of disorder is this? PTSD is a disorder that denotes one's failure to recover from a traumatic experience they may have witnessed or experienced. This condition is bound to last for months or even years, and although it seems like more of a mental disorder, it is accompanied by both emotional and physical reactions which can be extreme, as a result of triggers causing one to recall events that took place during their trauma. PTSD, however, requires a diagnosis from a medical professional. Symptoms can range from nightmares or flashbacks, anxiety, or a feeling of depression, to heightened reactions to things that provoke a response from one's organs or tissues in the body. The short-term and long-term effects of this disorder are; Behavioural changes (such as self-destructive behaviours or social isolation, getting easily irritated or angry),

Psychological effects (such as fear, extreme anxiety, and a lack or inability to trust others easily), Mood changes (for instance, a disinterest in activities the affected individual used to find pleasurable before the trauma, feelings of loneliness, guilt and shame), Detaching emotionally from loved ones or friends, and a Change in sleep patterns as a result of insomnia or nightmares.

Perpetrators can sometimes be considerate enough to use protection i.e., condoms while in the process of violating their victims, but what about those who just don't care enough to do so? That leads us to our next 'aftermath', which includes the risk of falling pregnant, accompanied by the risk of STIs, STDs, and HIV/AIDS. Now, these can't necessarily be isolated as they all are as a result of unprotected sex, thus I had to group them. First of all, when you engage with someone in a sexual activity such as sexual intercourse, protected or not, it is important that you are somewhat aware of your status, and theirs too, and I know what most individuals who are affected by some of the viruses or diseases I have just mentioned are thinking to themselves right now, "well, that cannot be true, I don't have to reveal my status to anybody", and I get you, I truly do understand how it feels to have yourself labelled and have people judge you based off of that, but that's not who you are, it isn't your identity and trust me, I am aware that not all of these diseases or viruses I have mentioned are only as a result of sexual intercourse, but they can be spread through sexual intercourse and so, if you have one stable sexual partner, then I do believe that you should not be selfish and try to protect your image while you might end up putting the life of another individual at risk. It is important to create a safe space to have conversations with your partner with regards to your sexuality, any issues or struggles you might be experiencing with your reproduction system, and any potential threats or risks that could affect your partner were they to engage in a sexual deed with you. But in cases of sexual assault such as rape, that advantage of being aware of the other individual's sexual history or patterns, let alone status, is not awarded to the victim, as it isn't even their decision to make, whether or not they want to engage in such an act, thus if protection isn't used, for example condoms or some form of contraceptives, then the victim might fall pregnant with the perpetrators seed, and honestly, it can never be an easy thing to accept and deal with, the baby will be a constant reminder of the victim's scars and trauma, their vulnerability in that moment during the assault, and it might be challenging for the victim to love and care for the baby(that's if they decide to keep him/her), without feeling like choking the baby or causing any harm to them every time they look at them because "your father did this to me", but that also does not mean that it is impossible to raise a baby who was conceived out of rape, one just needs to find the healing they need, see past their experience, and offer the baby the purest form of love they can because after all, aren't babies a gift from the Creator? However, if one chooses to not keep the baby and decide to abort instead, then that is their personal choice to make, and no one should put themselves in a position to judge them. On the same token, unprotected rape can result in the victim or the perpetrator being infected by STIs or STDs, now, I'm not going to tap on all these different kinds of diseases or infections that exist, you may use the internet, read articles or other books that mainly focus on this, to self-educate, I trust that you will get most of the answers you need. But I can perhaps list a few that are very common in both men and women, which are; HPV (human papillomavirus) also known as genital warts, Gonorrhoea, Chlamydia, Genital herpes(HSV), Trichomoniasis, Syphilis Hepatitis B and C (HBV /HCV), HIV(Human Immunodeficiency virus) and the Zika virus.

Moving right along, I present to you, the darkest of the darkest; depression and anxiety. Depression is a class of conditions that result in the rise or fall of an individual's mood. There are different kinds of depressions, and the most common ones being; clinical depression, persistent depressive disorder, Bipolar disorder, and postnatal depression, but in this book, we shall tap only into Clinical depression. Clinical depression is a mental health disorder and is a result of a constant feeling of sadness, a disinterest in various activities, new/old, important, and/or previously enjoyed by the depressed, thus causing the depressed individual to have little to no progress in their everyday life. Symptoms may include changes in sleep patterns, increase or loss in appetite, reduced or increased energy levels, loss of concentration causing slowness in activity, negative effects on self-esteem, etc. Depression is a very good friend of Suicide or suicidal thoughts rather, and the best way to treat this but isn't limited to; is through antidepressants, therapy, or both. Anxiety on the other hand will have your heart racing like a horse – heart palpitations, it will have you walking as if your feet are tied up together, or you are about to trip and fall over when you walk past a group of people; making you feel as though you could dig a hole for yourself and just hide in it never to come out, not to forget the endless breathe-ins and outs you need to make as you try to cool yourself down – panic attacks.

Nonetheless, the best way to treat all these conditions that I have mentioned above actually, is to seek medical attention and that includes therapy, medications, or medical procedures. An important note to make is that one should never self-diagnose, but rather seek medical attention and allow a medical professional to come to his/her conclusions, as they are more learned in this area.

After the rape, I wasn't doing so well. I had a loss of appetite, I was on ARVs for a month, disgusting! I suddenly felt as though I was choking on my own breath, and when I visited the doctor, he told me that I was suffering from what we call "Globus pharyngis", and as discussed before, it is a sensation that something is stuck in one's throat, and that is all due to the stress or anxiety caused by a sudden, shocking event in one's life. After a few visits at the doctor's office, he diagnosed me with all kinds of disorders, from PTSD, to anxiety disorder and depression, he said that he had no choice but to put me on chronic medication. "I am doomed", I thought to myself, "I hate medication!" Not to come off as though I am being insensitive towards persons with a positive HIV/AIDS status, or to those who use antidepressants, who have adopted this as a lifestyle, but because I just- I hate medication and I did not necessarily enjoy injecting what seemed like the whole pharmacy, every day into my body, plus, to make things worse, at a specified time. I mean my brain is such a potato, I can't even remember some of the things I say within the last two minutes of a conversation, now, having to remember taking medication every day at a certain time was just out of the question, I was doomed to fail at that, but thank goodness for alarm clocks because if it weren't for those, then I would most probably be sharing an entirely different story with you. I reeked of pharmaceuticals and that just made me even more sick, I felt like throwing up every two seconds, I had to force myself to eat to take the meds. From headaches, to feeling extremely fatigued, that became my norm. I was so angry, I could understand if I had put myself in this position, if I had initiated the sex which was unprotected, but that wasn't the case, I was raped and as a result, I had to go through all of this, and not him. His life went on perfectly fine, but I was stuck, emotionally. I was trapped, spiritually. I couldn't even get myself to pray, I just didn't know how to, not anymore. Every time I did, tears would just roll down my face, my eyes would become flooded, so it was hard, for the longest time, and I guess those tears became my prayers to God. I had a mental & spiritual block for what seemed like forever, I couldn't feel connected to God, not how I had been used to feeling, and I think that was my biggest mistake, putting a feeling as symbol of God's presence, because does it mean that when I don't feel that feeling any longer that, God is not with me? That, he's not comforting me, consoling me, or strengthening me?

Truth is; I would be lying if I said that I carried myself through all of this, yes, I did put in a lot of work, in bettering and healing myself, but the only way it would make sense to say that I had me, would be because I am one with God - Spirit, and with that same powerful breath in me, He strengthened me, He healed parts of me that were broken & shattered, He restored my peace, brought in me an incomprehensible joy.

However, I am not going to sit here and act as though the rape did not affect me, I know I have mentioned that one should never allow past negative experiences or the actions of other individuals towards them affect the person they become as they move forward, but the truth is; my encounter had me second-guessing my values and boundaries, like if I have been able to keep myself "contained" for so long, only to have someone come and take all of that away from me in a matter of minutes, was it even worth it anymore? I felt that I wanted to be in control, of every relationship that I got into. My boundaries were somewhat no longer existent. Even worse, I put myself in situations even though I knew they weren't for my highest good, all because of my trauma. I knew the good girl in me was wounded, she no longer was the girl she was before, her fairy tale, dreamland was destroyed by a man's weakness when it came to self-control and compassion, and she now wanted to express her strength through being, or rather feeling as though she was in control and not being taken advantage of, or being overpowered, by simply putting herself in situations that were not for her highest good. It isn't that she had no love or hope left inside her, I'm referring to myself right there; she was hopeful, she knew that although the world existed of imperfect humans who inflicted pain onto others, whether intentionally or unintentionally, still contained souls that were just as beautiful as her - light givers. She knew that the rape, although having scarred her, did not mean that her life was never going to turn out to be beautiful at some point, that the wound would never heal, and that she did not deserve to be loved and respected by a man, it just was hard for her to keep that hope when she kept encountering men who were nothing but triggers to what had happened to her before. Men who would not value her the way she valued herself, and knew she deserved to be valued, her encounters with such male species left her even more wounded because she struggled to put boundaries in place. Perhaps it was because she still needed to heal and feel whole again before she could pour out of her cup into another's, perhaps things had to get bad before they could get better because just like a seed, she needed to experience the darkness before she could fully be enlightened as she pierced through the layers of dirt, to fully bloom into who she was always meant to be, perhaps this was all a part of her story and she needed to learn a thing or two before she could fully operate in her fullness, as her highest self.

"I'm tired, tired of being strong. Life happens and you just have to be strong & continue. I need a break, just to gather myself up."
-The words of a survivor(Ms Rendy)

"At some point in life, you learn how to survive before you can start to live again."
-The words of a survivor(Ms Rendy)

But we've all fallen victim to one thing, or another at some point in our lives. It could have been childhood traumas or that had an impact (negative) on us in some way, or heartache caused by connections we have made with certain individuals, it could've been the loss of people we knew to be of value in our lives, which left us shattered; because it was sudden and unexpected, and we now are finding it hard to carry on living life without them. Perhaps it was or is something that has to do with family – family issues. Now, to take a step back, I hope you do realize that children are like sponges thus they absorb energy. So, if a child grew up in a household with some bad aura or vibes, chances are they inherit some of that energy and if not dealt with, carry it into their adulthood. But also, some struggles are just generational curses; you may have no idea how and why you are dealing with something and struggling to overcome it, but it might just be that it has been a cycle in your family, and although certain individuals may have gone through the same thing, they never dealt with the issue entirely thus it keeps hanging, the roots keep growing deeper and deeper into the soil(i.e. the foundation) and you might just be the only ground breaker, or root slasher of that cycle.

With that being said; with all these struggles we have fallen victim to, after certain experiences one has had, it can be a little challenging to pick oneself up and continue living as before, and this is where my judgement of other people has stopped. Because as much as one would like to, you know, "not let negative influences affect the way they carry themselves moving forward", the truth is that; experiences become part of our memories, because that is who we once were before, or that is what we have gone through before. Experiences shape us, whether positively or negatively, but you can't let past traumas and experiences dictate the way you carry yourself into the future, especially if your response to it becomes negative. You shouldn't give so much power to someone or something over your life. You must stand your ground! Keep holding onto your morals and values! Your foundation should be too strong to be shaken by any bad experiences, and if it is, it is never too late to build again.

However, the state of being on survival mode will leave you so guarded, that getting you to open up and be vulnerable all over again would require a wrecking ball to come crashing in on those walls, tearing them down, or a bulldozer to push through that large pile of dirt you've put up as a defence mechanism. But it isn't easy to deal with someone who is on survival mode, because they have been hurt and probably are still hurting, so trust doesn't come easy for them, they may even come off as being self-centred or egoistical, like all they are truly interested in is themselves and nobody else but that's just their survival skill, that's them learning to cope through the hurt and pain, before they can get back up on their feet again and start living, and not just existing.

What's my survival skill, you ask?

"Her softness keeps her sturdy on this rocky road called life."
-Ms Rendy

I have always found a way to channel my pain into creativity, to direct my pain to a greater cause, to allow myself to heal as I help

218

others heal too, and that's how I have been surviving. And I remain soft because soft does not break but hard does, think of the hardest object that you can think of and think of something even harder than that, and tell me that hard doesn't crack. But while you're at it, also think of softness, softness is gentle, it doesn't snap, softness is subtle, it rarely leaves a bend, and softness always bounces back.

I remain soft, and that just means kind, loving, and giving, because, in that sense, no one could ever take anything from me, it is by my own accord, to freely and willingly give, unlike when one is guarded and hardened up. When that person eventually decides to open up to someone and offer their love to that individual, best believe they will break or somewhat feel depleted when their love is rejected or mistreated by the other person because it was never in their character to give, they only did it for receipt.

And that is why no matter how many times I have been thrown around, juggled with, beaten down, stepped on, and scratched, I remain; soft, through it all, with the scars as signs that I have overcome.

CHAPTER 14- THE SWITCH UP

"But you can't let past traumas and experiences dictate the way you carry yourself into the future, especially if your response to it becomes negative."

-Ms Rendy

"You shouldn't give so much power to someone or something over your life. You must remain grounded. Grounded in your morals and values. Your foundation is too strong to be shaken by any bad experience", they say. But what happens when the way you were accustomed to things feels different now? Truth is that any trauma will have you switching up characters and expecting to go through something like that and return to how things were before the trauma, is rather unrealistic because there is a part of you that has left, not left as in "stayed behind", but left in the sense that "it is no longer there". There is a part of you that will always feel dead, you feel numb, and reality is a little disoriented for you. You are caught up between reality and this nightmare that keeps haunting you. The aftermath of such an experience(trauma) feels like living through Zombie land, you are physically presently here but you no longer feel like the You, you were before this. But either way, you continue to smile through each day, because although a part of you is no more, your arteries still pump honey and your soul still drips with that Golden Bee Syrup. You are still Golden. You've been to hell, and those few seconds there were traumatic for you, but you'll live through it, you have survived for a reason. Your light keeps beaming through that smile you give with hidden pain and insecurity deep within.

But the truth remains; that this kind of trauma(rape specifically) will leave you changed. You are going to try so hard to hold onto who you were before the incident, but you can't, and you pretty much are aware of that because you are not the same person, as a matter of fact, you've evolved so much because of the experience, and not to say that what happened to you was just or fair, or even necessary for your evolution, but to say that such experiences are there for learning and seeing the world with the naked eye, for what it truly is. The world is such a dark place, and that is why it takes a broken soul to still choose to illuminate it with its light, because when you've been hurt, you no longer look at the world with rose-coloured glasses, and choosing to still fall in love with life after you have been wounded just goes to show how much of a shining star you are, illuminating the path for anyone who might be struggling or dealing with trauma, depression, or anxiety from an experience such as yours.

Unfiltered notes;

It's been a few months down the line and for some reason, I thought I'd now be okay. That I would've had the whole experience out of my system, that thinking about it wouldn't hurt as much as did, but that's not how it be. If I had to be honest, I would probably let you know that it hurts, it hurts so much, so bad. Some days you are okay, and then on others, it all just comes crushing in, like suddenly you feel so torn apart, you wish you'd just forget, move on, and you try, but there are little reminders, or should I call them "triggers", that trap you into falling into that state, and as much as you don't want to go there, it is so hard not to think about it. So, you end up going back to that very same place that left you bruised, and every thought just brings your eyes into a waterfall-like state, your eyes become so teary, and you can't help but feel every emotion so deeply than you normally do. You try to make it stop, by pounding onto an object, or by choking yourself, just to not feel anything. Then it goes away, and you have to come back to reality, face the fact that you can't change it, it's happened, and it hurts, it freaking hurts.

But then again, you begin to realize that healing is a process, and accepting that you've been through such a traumatic encounter, and being in the know that it wasn't your fault, that the other individual's actions towards you were all on them, and that it had nothing to do with you, and choosing to forgive rather than to hold onto the pain and hurt even after you've sought justice from the criminal justice system and the court proceedings are taking a little longer than you expected, even though you have not received an apology for what has been done to you, you realize that closure has absolutely nothing to do with your perpetrator and that it has everything to do with you. You realize that to begin your journey onto this healing process, you need to release this person, release any anger and bitterness you might be holding against or towards them, because of the betrayal towards you. And you do this regardless of whether they offer you an apology or not. You might feel like confronting them, just to look them right in the eye and to ask them what their reason was for such gruesome behaviour towards you, especially because it was unprovoked. And you know what? It is okay for you to feel that way sometimes, especially in the initial stages of your healing process, because for some reason, you believe that if you get some form of an answer, it will help you move on. But what you don't realize at that moment is that you don't need to know why they did it, for you to be able to move on with your life. "Acceptance is the first step to your healing process".

But don't get me wrong when I say, "you do heal", because the truth is; healing is not a destination. Healing is not getting to a point where you entirely no longer feel the hurt or the pain, it's not getting to a point wherein you no longer are reminded of the terrible encounter or experience you have had. Healing is a sense of being at peace even when you come across triggers that remind you of the experience, it's knowing how to better deal with the negative emotions that uninvitedly surface and evade your space. It's being able to respond rather than to react when you are reminded of the situation, it's feeling every emotion, pain, and hurt and not being affected by it, but being able to handle it, and not to say that you dismiss it, but you allow yourself to feel every emotion deeply without having it entirely take control of you. Reaching a point of healing is "I know that this has happened to me, and it has become a part of my life story, but it doesn't necessarily define me, so I will not dwell on the negative side of the experience, but I will look at what the situation is here to teach me, I will take on the lesson and apply it to my life as I keep moving forward, limping, so as to not repeat the same mistake in the future, but to do better, to work on myself even more, because I do realise that there's so much more that lies ahead, beyond what has happened to me, but if I keep dwelling on the past, then I will miss out on the opportunity of the great things life still has to offer me, and that's all as a result of being in the know that in as much as life can be a harsh and terrible environment to find oneself in, life does have sacred moments where it will offer you more than what you had bargained for, and that is mainly because when it is your time, it will be your time, and the best way to describe it is by the quotation "Everything is divinely orchestrated".

I don't enjoy dining with a little pity for myself, neither do I daydream of dancing with my scars and pain, I know when people are watching this universe like it's from out of space, from that telescopic view, they might think they have zoomed into every aspect of this planet, but that sight they get from looking from the outside offers only a glimpse of its surface. There's so much more to this planet that is yet to be uncovered, because until people dig a little deeper into the surface, through the crust layer, and remove the rocks and dirt piled up to protect this bone structured, flesh wrapped, spirit dominated vessel, all they will ever see is the beauty of its surface, and unfortunately never its core, crying and erupting with pain, fear, shame, and insecurities. They will never get to see the beauty of its core, i.e., the serene peace it experiences after a storm has erupted the entirety of its emotions. They will never experience the intensity of its love, and so, just like mother earth, they will judge it from its surface, if it isn't green enough then it must lack beauty, it must lack life and growth, but the truth is trauma has you switching up your personality real quick. The depression associated with trauma(i.e., Post-traumatic stress disorder) isn't always going to look like sadness and darkness that people often assume it does, sometimes you are going to find a coping mechanism, and for me, it was always masking my deep, intense feelings in respect of my trauma, with humour, not that I wasn't confronting my demons, I did, I was, but mostly when I was alone. Every chance I got to be alone, I used that to confront my emotions and hurt, I would use that time to nurture them, embracing them but not drowning my soul in them. One thing I have learnt about being emotionally strong wasn't that one is "able to hide their emotions and pain well", but it was that they are able to confront their emotions, nurse them, hence emotionally strong individuals have control over their emotions and not the other way round. Control in the sense that they allow themselves to feel, when it's time to get emotional but they don't constantly throw themselves pity-parties and dwell in their sadness for unnecessary amounts of time, they know when it's time to cry and when it's time to move on from the pain, that is control".

If you've been through life's mess, your soul breaks a little. On some days I feel a little beyond repair like my soul has been shattered but the bit of hope that's left in me keeps me up on my feet, dragging me along through life's path, to keep pushing through, till the finish line.

I cannot lie and say I have been doing okay all this while, or from the beginning. I remember feeling this way just a few days post my sexual assault encounter;

Very Unfiltered Notes:

"My life is shitty right now and no one really understands! I wish all this could just end, that I'd be gone when I wake up the next day and didn't have to deal with any of this. All they tell me is 'you have just got to be strong', 'it will all be okay', 'you are strong, a very strong individual'. And maybe right now I'm not, or I perhaps don't feel that way, maybe it doesn't feel as though I'm going to be OK, as though anything will be okay. I am trying to move on, to push myself out of this hell hole and well, I know people are trying to help and they are trying to do the best they can, but it feels like none of them are, this mess is mine to deal with and they make it heavier when they are always on my case, in my face, asking if 'I'm ok!?' That's what he asked me after he messed with my whole life! He asked if I was okay, if what he was doing was okay, and although I said no, he continued, continued to take from me, to ruin all parts of my soul. Now I'm shattered, day by day I feel like I'm coming to the end of myself. I just cannot deal with this. I'm trying very hard to forget what happened, to focus on what I came here for, but every moment feels like crap! Every part of my soul is breaking. I'm tired, I'm exhausted. I just need to rest, God, you surely know that! But still, you allow everything to not go my way. Everything is messed up and it feels as though you're just watching from heaven like my life's a movie, and although deep down I know you're with me and for me, I fail to believe that sometimes! You know what hurts? To know that this guy gets to move on with his life. He gets to roam around freely, while I'm scared, to show he doesn't regret and care what he's done and about me, he got himself a lawyer, to come save him from this shitty mess he created. He should've just killed me, like most of them do when they are done taking what's not even theirs. I walk anxiously, scared he might show up and take my life, oh how I wish he did it then because honestly, that evening I felt a part of me die. But had he not just killed my soul but my physical Being, I believe I wouldn't have to deal with any of this. He wouldn't have to deal with this too. He would've just disposed of my remains somewhere, where no one would find me, I guess I'd be at rest then. I know there's so much that lies ahead of me, dreams and goals, a purpose but I feel like he should've just taken it all".

This was me, tired, raw, f'd up, and exhausted.

And I know how many people who have lost their daughters or loved ones in such an event, may feel that I'm privileged to have been offered a chance to carry on with life, and to continue to fulfil my life's purpose, to continue to chase after my dreams, goals, and passions, but if I'm being truthful; it isn't that I am unappreciative of that, I mean, I thank God daily for that opportunity, but it gets heavy sometimes, to a point where I feel that being dead would have been so much better; that way I wouldn't have to deal with any emotions and/or have to relive that moment as it replays in my head. Do you want to know how I feel about him? I mean, you would expect me to hate him, but all I feel is compassion towards him, and it has nothing to do with the fact that we may have somehow "bonded" in some form of sexual activity. I can't help but wonder what he's struggling with; Did he experience molestation during his childhood, like me? What was the issue? Was it because he was grieving his wife? Maybe the pain was just too much to bear that it led him to losing control of his mind. Was he perhaps struggling with the issue of pornography? Perhaps he had been addicted to it to the point where he wanted the experience for himself, and he couldn't contain his urges any longer? Was I perhaps the problem? Did I make him want to lose all his self-respect and respect towards me because of how I was dressed? I wasn't even wearing anything too revealing though or was I just an easy target? – self-blame. Perhaps he is just a narcissist, and he gains some form of satisfaction and control from inflicting pain onto others and seeing them hurt because that makes him feel superior.

Before the encounter, I used to think that you have to forgive someone or that forgiveness should only be offered when, or if someone has apologised. I used to believe that if someone who has hurt me or done me wrong never apologised to me, then that meant that I need not move past what they have done to me. But then the rape happened, I encountered a terrible incident with a particular individual, they hurt me badly, their behaviour towards me, in my opinion, was just unforgivable, given the kind of 'relation' we had, and the fact that they initiated their actions towards me, unprovoked. I was a little bitter at first, I mean who wouldn't be? But I'm grateful for the small circle of supportive friends and family I had at the time, they honestly held me together when I was falling apart, they picked me up and that for me was the purest kind of love I have ever experienced.

So, here's The Wisest Advice on Forgiveness I Got from the encounter:

"Learn to separate a person from their actions."
You know why? Because people do things, very terrible things, but that doesn't mean that they are terrible people. Sometimes, people are genuinely good people, they are respectable, and have good morals and values, but some circumstances may occur that lead them astray and lead them into "committing" actions that they wouldn't necessarily have committed, under normal circumstances, but forgiving them does not mean that you excuse their behaviour, no, but what it does mean is that you realize that they are human just like you, and that every single one of us is capable of making stupid mistakes in life as a result of our bad

229

decision-making, but we all deserve second chances, only if we will step up to the table/plate and take responsibility and accountability for our actions, and actively work towards becoming and doing better. And even if the person is not remorseful in any way(because some people are sick like that), you still realize that there is a darkness out here in this world, that they might be trapped in a dark space with little, or no light coming through, but you choose to illuminate it with your light, by forgiving them, and you also realize that you don't have the time and energy to carry along with you 'baggage' that will only weigh you down and hinder you from fully becoming all that you are meant to be, so still you choose to forgive them, not only for them, but for you, because you deserve that peace, and you deserve to move on with your life and focus on better.

Sometimes it's hard to accept that a "good" person could do a terrible thing, and even harder to see them having to face the repercussions that come with that action, but it's necessary. Because the truth is, everything in life is a choice, and every single one of us must account for our actions.

In as much as the encounter taught me how to forgive, it wasn't that I had been one who found it hard to forgive, I have never been one who struggled with forgiveness, but I can admit that I do however struggle with forgetting.

So, what is forgiveness then, you ask? Forgiveness can't be forced; it isn't something that happens overnight. Stop trying to force people to get to a point of forgiveness towards you just because you are "sorry". Allow people to feel whatever they need to feel before they reach a state of release of their negative harboured emotions & feelings towards you. Someone who knows that they are in the wrong will humble themselves and accept whatever the wronged individual's response to their actions is, because at some point, the wronged individual was in a place where they too were very accepting of the lies, deceit, or hurtful actions without even being aware of that. Also, just because someone forgives you, it doesn't mean that you are guaranteed access into their life. An individual could forgive you but never want to be associated with you ever again, and that is okay. Forgiveness isn't forgetfulness, truth is; the betrayal, lies or whatever wrongdoing that was there will always stick around. Forgiveness is giving grace, knowing what someone is capable of doing because of their history record, but still choosing to give them a chance to coexist with you in harmony, regardless of what they have done, see? It's not that I don't know what you have done, it isn't that I have forgotten, no, I am fully aware of what you are capable of doing, but I give you grace because hearts & souls that are willing to change still do exist, but then there are some that just aren't evolved enough to be open to change, resulting in the same results still being produced even after a second chance has been granted, but that is not on me but on them. And, because in terms of the law of attraction, negative vibes(energies) attract negative vibes, holding onto negative harboured emotions or feelings will only result in the attraction of such negative energies in one's life, therefore, why would I want to put my peace, joy, and life in jeopardy all because of an individual who has done me wrong, who probably does not even care about what goes on in my life anyway? See, forgiveness is giving, giving chance after chance even when someone struggles or chooses to not do right by you. I would like to share with you the biggest realisation that I had on forgiveness, on a random day, while I was in my train of thoughts. Just so you know, I'm the kind of person to note or jot things down, just so I don't forget or perhaps it's because my mind is too preoccupied because of my overthinking tendencies, that I might lose an idea in a swamp of thoughts. So, while I was in my thoughts, I got an image of how holding on to grief, strife or anger looked like in God's eyes; it was a picture of boxing gloves, now, imagine yourself wearing boxing gloves and going before The Giver in prayer, asking for blessings, to receive more and then leaving and feeling as though nothing has changed in your life. Not to say that everything you ask for will immediately be afforded to you, of course timing and alignment are important aspects to consider, but inner peace will always be experienced whether one receives whatever they have requested or not. On that note, if you don't get where I'm going with this, take a deep breath and let's try again, as this is simple to understand;

When we go before The Giver in prayer, holding so much anger and strife in our hearts, holding grudges over other people, literally looks like the image I've just explained above(wearing boxing gloves). You pray and ask God to enlarge your territory, with more, and God blesses you, he surely pours out His blessings unto you, but you see how one can't necessarily hold anything while wearing boxing gloves? It is so with us, as the blessings pour out of the Givers hands into yours, they slip off your hands because you are holding onto the unnecessary, you miss your blessings because you are already holding onto what God has not allocated in your hands! But if you take off those gloves, in literal terms; "if you let go of that grief or anger", watch how light your hands(heart in other words) become, how easy it is to carry so much in your hands, the blessings of God, that is". So, forgiveness can be defined as an act of letting go, releasing any ill-thoughts, anger, strife, or grief towards any person who may have intentionally or unintentionally caused harm to you, or anyone close to you. But as mentioned before, I do not struggle with forgiving people, I always find it easy to release and let go of anger, but one thing I find challenging is forgetting, therefore, if you play me dirty, the chances of me ever fully "naively" trusting you again are close to a nil, and the reason why I say "close to a nil" and not necessarily "just a nil" is because I give people chances, I do believe in people changing for the better, however, if you think you're smart & funny, and can step on my toes as you wish because you think I'm "stupid or too soft", then RIP to you.

But even so, I have come to a point of realisation in my life, that not everyone I meet is, or will be emotionally or spiritually inclined, meaning that knowledge or wisdom that may come easy to me may not necessarily come easy for them, in layman's terms; some people are still going to be a little immature than me, they are still going to lack that emotional intelligence, still may be going through a long journey of self-discovery, learnt lessons, and Maturity, therefore I should not always take things personal, especially when it comes to how others treat me.

I've read so many times that "the way people treat you is based off of what you allow", which is sometimes true but also always isn't, and here's what I mean by that; the first time you meet a person, they will treat you how they feel is right and also depending on the kind of energy you exude, as time goes on and you get comfortable around them, you may set boundaries letting them know what you will tolerate and how far is too far. But even though you set those boundaries, some people may still choose to not respect those boundaries, now, does that mean that you are allowing them to treat you that way or is it that they are just disrespectful? See, sometimes people treat you based on who they are, or how they feel about themselves, and that has got nothing to do with you. A liar will lie to you because they are untruthful, a cheater will cheat on you because they are immature, lack loyalty and have no respect for themselves, the person they are cheating on and also the person they are cheating with, a bully could throw negative comments to someone else because they maybe do not feel confident enough in themselves, and want to bring someone else's confidence low to their level just so they aren't alone in their miserable insecure level. However, the problem isn't always the other person, it could also be that you allow people to overstep boundaries you have created, and disrespect you because maybe you haven't matured enough to set healthy boundaries and to keep them in place regardless of who comes into your life, but then again, it could also be that there is absolutely nothing wrong with you, and that the individuals who treat you badly are just insecure, lying , immature douchebags, or they are literally just projecting. Either way, you should never take anything that's coming from someone else that does not resonate with your soul or who you are, personal.

CHAPTER 15- BEHOLDEN TO GRACE

I am grateful for the chance to still be able to continue to fulfil my dreams and goals, but I just- it's really stressing me out, to think of everything, the encounter, trying to forget, daily, I won't lie, it has been extremely hard, truly hard. Some days I wake up and just want to not feel at all, no emotion whatsoever.

If I had to be bare face honest with you, I would let you know that I have tried to get myself to meet the end of me. I have felt the urge, it was scary yet so real, it felt as though it was time. I have tried to end me, it was nothing dark and intentional like that, I just wanted to numb the pain, it was so innocent yet so brutal, but I thank God for granting me grace by giving me self-control.

How do I explain the feeling to you? It all started with a thought, there must've been something that triggered me, and when that happened, I found myself thinking of how it all went down, from his touch, to how I wanted him to stop so bad but he just wouldn't, I began to tear up, a drop ran down my left cheek (you know how people usually say the harm or hurt must've been painful if you cry with your left eye first, or something along those lines). And then, suddenly, it felt as though a storm was raging inside of me, I was mad, mad-angry because I couldn't get the answers I wanted -why me? I rushed to the bathroom to look myself right in the mirror, perhaps seeing myself would help calm the storm, but seeing that girl, broken and wounded inside, led to an explosive volcano of tears. I kept gasping as I tried to catch a breath in the middle of tearing up. I made things worse, seeing her, myself, in that mirror just made me feel terrible for still being here, disgusted for what I had allowed to happen to such a beautiful soul, unwillingly. I rushed back into my bedroom, avoiding any eye contact with any object that would reflect my image. I shut the door closed, stood right at the door holding the door handle as tightly as I could, with my body against the wall, I began to glide, downwards, as I continued to tear up, I couldn't help but let out some heavy breathing as I let go of the door handle, I finally found myself sitting on the floor, and the next thing that happened shocked me; I reached in for my neck with both hands, I squeezed, in hopes to numb the feelings I felt at the time, and it sure felt good, shifting the focus from my emotional pain, to a more physical pain, but choking myself? I stopped immediately when I felt like I was about to run out of breath. Was it worth it, the short-term pleasure of pain-numbing?

I mean, I wasn't suicidal, I had never been, I did not know of any suicidal trends in my family history, and I for sure wasn't trying to be suicidal, it was just a coping mechanism for me, one that I would never recommend to anyone. Being suicidal is different, this means that you strategically plan your own ending, this is a mental decision one makes, it's a thought out process on "how I am going to end my life", from going to a supermarket to purchase a rope to hang oneself, finding the right spot to hang ones neck to, finding the perfect chair to position ones feet on, and calculating the timing of when to kick the chair to allow one's body to freely hang off from the ceiling or some tree in the backyard, to going to a local drugstore, standing in a long queue with other very much alive individuals to purchase loads of tablets and returning home only to use every one of those meds to end one's life, swallowing every pill down ones throat, I mean, I don't even enjoy taking medication when I am truly sick, it truly must be that deep, and very thought out. If I had to come up with my own definition of suicide it would be "an intentional act to end oneself, to bring oneself to one's finale, to the end because of the inability to cope and continue on the journey of life as a result of something threatening that may have happened to one or may have been caused by one", suicide is a reaction to an unbearable situation, that "I'm tired and just don't know what to do with myself", that "there's just no other way out of this mess, life's mess" – escapism, suicide is like a coping mechanism, just that in this case it leads to the event of death, and upon that event you do not have to continue living through each day, experiencing the pain of just feeling numb, confused and tired, at least not on this earth. It is a chance to escape to somewhere better, the hope of finding a better place to start afresh or to just rest, a plea for a fresh start in this life thing, even if it is in an entirely different sphere, and that is just how scary it is. I imagine what truly is going on in ones thought process, that makes them reach that decision to end their own life, to have been pushed so further onto the edge that you have nowhere else to turn to but the grave?

I won't lie, sometimes I have days where I just want to throw in the towel, to give up and give in to defeat, because I will honestly be feeling tired, extremely exhausted, and not the physical kind. But when I look back to where I've been? To what I've been able to pull myself through, and out of? I tear up because God! He's been so damn good through all this chaos, and I can't let all that grace go to waste just because of how I am feeling. I mean, of course life can be shitty sometimes, and it will have you feel like throwing in the towel, have you wanting to ask for a pause, want to rewind, reminisce, and stay in previous chapters, but that isn't possible. Life will throw you with sword after sword, life will keep taking, breaking, tearing up, and shattering your 'oh so fragile' soul and you will still be left with having to show up daily, and continue to live through this thing called life. Some days will feel like a breeze, while other days will seem like you are trying to escape from the terror of this horror movie of a life, but you know what's beautiful about life? Every chapter is fucking beautiful, in the messiness, the confusion and hardships, strength becomes prevalent, patience is born, compassion and love towards others & self, is grown, and that for me is absolutely beautiful. The beauty of life lies in persevering, in being hopeful through not only the good days but also the toughest of times, because life is about learning, and growing, and reaching fulfilment. It is about the in-between fun that's shared with other Beings, the weird but intriguing conversations that are had with random strangers, the little moments and things that seem unimportant, and that's my reason to keep going.

Unspoken words.

To the Rapist, Abuser, Liar, User, and Murderer;

What went wrong? I am aware that this thing (Rape/Abusive/Polygamy Culture) has been going on for ages now, but what I am trying to figure out is where it all started. What gives you the right to do something so horrendous to another Being? I am a firm believer of men being the Knight in shining armour of our women, you guys being the ones to provide and care for us, but not showing entitlement, rather equality and mutual respect. But lately it's been the complete opposite. Instead of providing, all you do is take and steal from us. Instead of protecting, you provoke, you hurt us, showing no remorse for your actions towards us.

What went wrong?

I am pleading on behalf of every single woman, child, mother, daughter, sister, girlfriend, aunt, and wife, on behalf of every FEMINAL BEING and ANYONE who has ever been hurt by a man, that you please make us understand what the issue is?

Is it so fulfilling to see us wrecked, broken, butchered and bruised!? Do you not care much about us? What have we done to deserve such gruesome behaviour?

Secondly, I have a request:

Would you please just stop now? We have had enough! We are tired and exhausted, not just physically but emotionally too. This constant fear that we live in is stealing our freedom away from us. Do you not know that we are equals!? Created by one God and given the same power and authority? We just want a life where we can coexist with men and not feel threatened by them or vice versa. We want peace, we need it! Respect is at the top of our request list. But also, can you all redefine the concept of manhood or masculinity? This man filled with ego and so much pride, lust for power and control, this abusive, self-righteous, and self-seeking man, who is he? Where does he come from? What happened to the ever so loving, Respectful, caring, and protective man - our leader!? Where is he? Because we need him. Bring him back! Set him free! And I can understand it's a little frustrating for the Man who is nothing like that, but I'm sorry that your gender has put you in this kind of position, in a position where your credibility has been tarnished, you have to work twice as hard to earn our trust, but in times where women may come off as a little aggressive and too demanding because they cannot take any more of the pain, I ask of you to not sit back and label them as being loud and unnecessarily seeking attention, because as unfair as it may be for you, it is really up to you to change the narrative of what manhood has for long been defined as.

Lastly, I cannot reiterate this enough; WE ARE TIRED AND EXHAUSTED! Also, this is coming from a sincere place, we want our men back! Not these violent, self-satisfying, power-seeking creatures that we have no idea from where they come. WE NEED OUR MEN!

P. S Please heal!

To the first man who stole my innocence;

Do I say I hate you? Or is hate such a strong word to use? You stole from me, exposed me to things that a child my age should never have been exposed to. You trapped me, trapped me in an endless cycle of addictions which is so hard to end or escape from. I feel robbed of a childhood that consists of only things that children do i.e. play games with other kids, eat, laugh, go to school and just be a kid, because you burdened me with baggage that not even an adult can carry, you poisoned me, poisoned my soul with ivy causing a reaction of fear & shame whenever I was around other people. But I do sit and wonder how it truly feels to be a child without having been exposed to the "adult world". How it feels to be a child still with your innocence wrapped up around you, because I've never had that, or well, I did but only for a short while.

But even so, I release the anger and the shame I have carried around all because of what you did to me. I forgive you, whether you have apologised or not. And I pray that your soul too be released from the bondages of addictions as mine was, and I pray that if you did feel any guilt over what you did to me, that you learn to forgive yourself too.

To my perpetrator;

Where do I begin? Do I tell you of how I truly never thought that you would do such a thing to me and how angry I felt after you had betrayed my trust by violating my pride and privacy? Or do I tell you of the bruising I felt from the touch of the hands of a man who laid hold of every part of me that I had known for so long to be sacred? Do I remind you of the multiple opportunities you were presented with to say no to your urge of fulfilling your selfish desires but instead you chose to ignore them? Or do I tell you of the aftermath of your actions towards me? Repercussions...

I'm hurt. Not hurt because of the stares you gave me while you were busy calculating your course of action towards me, not because of the physical pain you inflicted through the touch of your hands as you caressed and seduced every curve and corner of my body, no! I am wounded, and this kind of wound goes beyond just the violation you had on the physical parts of my body, it's emotional, it's spiritual, it's that deep. My soul is heavy, burdened by the betrayal, confusion, and unanswered questions as to why you did what you did and why it had to be me. It haunts me every single day of my life. I'm hurting and I can't help but wonder if you ever sit alone and think to yourself "what have I done to her?". Do you ever wonder how I am doing? Do you even care? Now I have a burden of trust issues and insecurities embedded deep inside me because I cannot look at another human being and not think of what you've done to me and the possibility of them doing the same thing to me again. I cannot get intimate and that's literally not being able to let anyone get too close to me because I'm too scared, afraid that if I let them in they might just hurt me like you did and I will be left with the responsibility of having to heal a wound that I had no hand in creating, a wound that was caused by another Man who lacked the integrity and compassion, or empathy for another MAN. Now I walk around with my guard up because my trust was once broken. I am constantly in my head because I want to know why? Why you did it? Why me? Was I that vulnerable? An easy target perhaps? Do you feel sorry? For what happened? Am I the first? Will it happen again? How am I supposed to face you? What were you thinking? What's going on in your head right now? Are you Ok? Were you that tempted? That you couldn't hold yourself. Well, that is not an excuse though. But Why? Just why? I cannot say I know what it is that made you do what you did to me, But what I can tell you is how it made me feel, not that I expect to get an apology from you, not because I want to be pitied by you, I do not care about whether or not you are remorseful about what you've done to me, well at least at this point, I used to fuss so much over whether or not you thought of me, whether you cry the same tears I let out because of the ravage you've caused inside of me, but not anymore. I have come to learn that it is necessary to forgive, not for you as my perpetrator, but for me, for my own peace.

To the boy I thought I loved;

It was never just a mind thing, I truly loved you, and you hurt me. I gave all that was left in me, and you - you betrayed me. I could never go back to how things were, I can't unsee you for the person you've shown me. You brought out the worst in me and I allowed you to. I'll admit, I was toxic too. I am not going to sit here and play victim. I have tried to give you a taste of your own medicine through my bitter words and cold acts towards you in hopes that that would wound your soul too, just like you did mine. I take responsibility for my actions, but I could never go down for the choices and mistakes that you've made. I cannot wish the worst on you, because even with the worst that you brought out in me, you brought the best too, and for that, I am grateful. I've convinced myself that it's best to move away from this connection because I don't feel valued/respected enough and that's owing to your actions, but deep down I cannot help but wish that it would be you & I in the end. Am I selfish? For hoping that you choose me and not any other woman? That you drop everyone else just for me, even if it means it'll hurt them? Am I perhaps stupid for believing that what we had was real even though the facts could prove that it was all just a lie? Is it unfair of me to want to put all the blame on you for how things turned out even if I knew from the start that it wasn't going to end well but still chose to stay? Am I being inconsiderate for thinking of you as being the same as every other guy?- playa, selfish, dodgy for not wanting to face the music because it feels like you avoid the truth at all cost and you just want to look out for yourself? Am I a little crazy for missing you so damn much but also wanting to

cuss at you because I'm so mad? Like I can't get over
the fact that you looked at me right in the eye, not
once but most of our time together and blatantly lied,
why did you continue being with me, let alone 'entangle'
knowing that you still were tied up elsewhere? Was it to
have me stuck on you too? Maybe I'm being too
emotional about this and overthinking too much about
it, But Would I be wrong to say that you are being
selfish for wanting me to stay but still not wanting to
commit to only me? To say that I kind of feel used, even
though you keep telling me that I'm this amazing
person, with a great personality and that it's me you
want? For feeling as though you're choosing someone
else even though you say it is me that you want,
because of your indecision? For thinking that you saying
that you are confused is just an excuse for not wanting
to choose because "if you truly wanted me you would've
made sure you cut all lose ends just to be with me"? Am
I too dreamy and naïve for wanting to believe that this
should've flowed so easily without any challenges,
especially in the beginning? Because we had only just
started though... Perhaps I should just leave like I said
I was, because I might just come off as being
desperate, but why do I miss you so damn much? I miss
the excitement I'd get every time I knew I was going
to see you, I miss touching you, and feeling you so close
to me even when we were not doing anything bizarre,
but just sitting & holding each other. I miss how we'd
exchange deep breaths underneath every kiss because
that's how passionate we felt about each other. I can't
help but miss how you always wanted to make fun of me
and then act all mad because you don't like it when the
tables turn and I'm the one who's laughing. I miss

talking to you about anything without forcing the conversation, I miss how you randomly would want to act like a baby from the way you spoke to just the way you wanted to be held by me -Reminiscing. I just miss you and that annoys me a lot, because when I look back, I can't help but think of all the times I got signs that something was off and I ignored them, and even though I can sit here and reminisce over those few moments we had together, I know the situation isn't going to change and there's absolutely nothing that I can do about it, so I guess this is me saying goodbye, releasing and forgiving the past.

To my scars;

I thank you, for being a part of my journey. I welcome you and accept you with no judgement, I embrace every single one of you. You have brought me each of both sides, the good and the bad. The joy, and the pain. The laughter and the tearing up half-way through the smiles. You are my little reminders, of how strong I am and how strong I have become. Of how much magic is contained in my bones, to revive a soul that was once shattered and broken, into this beautiful Creature who sparks stardust everywhere she goes, that I, am pure light in my darkness.

CHAPTER 16- DOES IT GET ANY BETTER?

"But wait, you thought that it would be a happy ending, didn't you? Well, it is but not the way that you may be envisioning it. Rilonde gave, she gave it her all in love, but every guy was nothing short of the previous guy who betrayed her love & trust, and/or took it for granted, as he was just an upgraded version of each player at the game of love & life. And so, she felt hurt, betrayed, disappointed and disrespected, she questioned what was so wrong with her that every guy wanted her but never wanted to stick around, why she attracted deceiving, selfish men who pretended to love her when they still were messing around with other women. And maybe it wasn't that they were pretending to 'love' her, maybe they did, love her, but just had a different perception of what love meant, because for her; love required a certain level of respect & care, to not cross boundaries, and to not intentionally cause pain.

But perhaps that's the thing with love; Love is selfless, and while she expected everyone else to give to her the way that she did, she needed to understand that that wasn't how love and life worked. See, love does not have expectations, it is meant to flow effortlessly out of one's core, love does not have conditions, that "I will give to you only if so and so happens", no, love gives, it gives chance after chance, not because it is so blinded it doesn't see through the games and deceit, but love gives even when it sees the faults presented to it, love isn't changing, feelings grow hence they

250

fluctuate, but love is constant in the way that it gives, it is not hindered or influenced by outside influences, it remains even after it has been betrayed. Don't get me wrong when I say that love remains or stays even after it's been betrayed, because no one should ever tolerate bad behaviour or any form of disrespect or toxicity all because they love someone, in fact, love isn't all about being physically present in someone's life, it isn't about allowing oneself to be abused and used all in the name of "patience", sometimes love requires one to take a step back and allow for the receiver of love to deal with their own demons alone, to learn and to grow - alone, and not that love won't be present then, it will, but just because you are out of someone's life it doesn't mean that your feelings for that person still do not run deep, they do, but you stop putting in the effort into that connection because your love deserves to fall into the hands of a receiver who will truly appreciate it and not take it for granted. Love is gentle, patient and so understanding, it is never rushed, and that is why love should never be forced, because as mentioned already, it is meant to flow effortlessly out of one's core, into another. Giving isn't such a bad thing as we make it to be, I know it hurts to give love and have your love rejected, it freaking sucks, but it isn't that your love is not enough, it isn't that there is something wrong with your love. Love can be frightening, because instead of tossing another away and condemning them of their faults, love covers one around and soothes their fears and feelings of shame, love is accepting, love goes deeper into one's soul and causes a surface of emotions, and because being emotional requires vulnerability, love scares away those who can't be raw, open, and honest with not only others, but themselves.

251

She was a beam of light, they were attracted to that, the hope, the joy, the peace, and the love, they lacked that and could sense that she possessed such from their connections with her, but because they themselves were not on her level, she made them feel a little insecure as she wore her heart on her sleeves, she was never afraid to live and speak her truth, while they could only try to live up to that version of her. But see, the thing about romantic love is that it involves a union between two persons, two different, flawed (one loves soccer, the other does not get it, one enjoys mingling with other persons while the other would rather stay at home in their slouchy lounge-wear and read a good book) individuals. Romantic love is about finding a common denominator, reaching a common ground, it is about choosing one individual who matches with your soul and choosing to stick with them, not because there aren't other individuals who are catchy to your eye, but because there exists a level of mutual respect and care between you and the person you have chosen.

Love is selfless and I believe the only reason why relationships fail is because humans are selfish. If love existed between two selfless Beings, there would be no need for disappointment in love. And maybe we do not understand the concept of compromise fully, because while you are thinking that compromise means changing up who you are, or giving up all or most of what you are to fit into someone else's life or world, compromise simply means abandoning one's lower vibrations that may cause hindrances in one's connection with another, because love will never require you to leave any part of yourself behind unless of course it was never for your highest good."

-Ms Rendy

Perhaps I'm the problem, perhaps I'm too demanding of a love that the human heart cannot give, perhaps my idea of love being this selfless act that one shows to another, is not how everyone else views it. Perhaps my notion of love being a choice, and it being about choosing that one soul that one will stick with forever is just that - an idea, which would explain the endless disappointments I've had in love, from individuals who weren't willing to explore this act of choice with me. But I wonder, is my love too idealistic for the reality that we live in, or are more and more individuals becoming too 'realistic' that they forget that reality is in itself an ideal? That it is what we make of it from our own ideas and beliefs of what the world is, and dreams of how we'd like for it to be? But even so, my idea of what love is remains; an act of altruism towards another, through choice.

And so, I met someone, he spoke to the very depths of my Being, "I love you" he whispered right into my ear, I felt the very emotion that came with those words and every time I just - I would just lose myself completely in those perfectly constructed words and his deep vibrational sounding voice "I love You even more", I'd say, burying my face right into his chest. But I remember one particular day when that had happened and he held the side of my head, lifting and turning it towards his, and starred right into the windows of my soul - my eyes, "I know you've been through so much pain, and I never want to put you through the very same things you've been through." It was those very words that made me want to forget about my past hurts and pain, he spoke to my trauma, reminded it that it had no power over me, he made me feel that it was okay to heal and still feel sadness every now and then.

I felt safe to speak to him about what everyone was referring to as "the incident", he had a healing aura that came with him, made my fears & anxiety succumb to the joy that he rekindled in me - Light, he was (or so I thought), he shined it to every part of my Being that was ever wounded. It hurt, facing the truth, being honest with myself about still requiring more time to heal. I wanted to move on, badly, but I also realised one thing; Healing does not require isolation, love heals, being surrounded by people who bring out the light in you is part of healing, I didn't have to not put myself out there because I was hurting or pained.

I could still be healing and have myself fall in love again, and of course, establishing new relations while you still carry emotional baggage from the past isn't healthy at all, plus I have already made a point in one of the previous chapters, of having to detach from any negative or bad habit that disallows one to operate as their highest Self, but let's not forget what healing truly is, it is a process, and life doesn't stop until you are in a place where you feel better and feel that you can participate again, not to say that you have to purposely get into relationships even though you're still feeling a little broken because "they will heal you", but healing does not have a timeline and also, healing is different for everyone. For me, healing is realising the wound that was caused in you and actively working towards ameliorating it. Your life does not have to be on a standstill because of one minor or even major setback. I wasn't going to give power to someone who was not making any contribution to my life – my perpetrator or the ghost that had unexpectedly disappeared from my life. He may have wounded me, but I had survived. I am a survivor, and I am proud of it! I have had sleepless nights in hopelessness, thinking and feeling that I was coming to the end of me, there have been times where I wanted to end this, I thought it would be better to close this chapter sooner, thinking that I would forget about the experience, the whole of it, but I'm still here.

After the pain, I remained guarded. I could not just loosen up to every or anyone who showed up at my life's doorstep. Trust, like respect, is earned. But was I too closed off?

After a few months had gone by, I met this guy. He looked just okay, had a chilled, laid back vibe to him. We met at the food market where I had gone to pick up a few items to add to my grocery. I saw him gaze at me with excitement, but I wasn't interested in any way, I mean, my heart was still in tremendous pain, and I felt that our interaction would lead to more than just a Hello - Goodbye encounter, but he was so determined to speak to me. He came over to the fruits section and pretended to be picking some, but I could see right through his acting. "Hello", he said, I responded with a "Hi", making sure to not make any eye contact as I picked some grapes and bananas, and pushed the trolley rather fast, whilst walking away from his midst.

I may have lost him for a while, or so I thought. I proceeded with my shopping, picking up a few snacks, Fritos chips & some Oreo chocolate biscuits, a favourite of mine. I then went over to the till to pay, after having picked up some other items as well. The whole time I made sure I had my phone out, with the calculator App open to estimate how much everything would cost. Having arrived at the till, the lady assisting me was sure to scan everything and to my surprise, my calculations were off by just 20 bucks, meaning that the money I had in my bank account just wasn't enough, but a huge coincidence was that the same gent that I had met prior, was somehow the person who stood behind me in line, and guess what he did? He offered to pay for everything. However, as guarded as I had become, because of the rape, deceit, and heartache, I was not going to allow him to do that. So, I only agreed to him paying the outstanding balance, which was approximately R22 and a few cents, he paid and offered to give me a lift to my place as well, because I was carrying a handful of bags. I wanted to say no but thought it would be a great opportunity to get to talk to him and get his details just so I could pay him back his money.

We went to the parking lot, I was nervous, because here I was entering into a strange man's car, I didn't know him, I've had some terrible encounters in my life, the trauma still haunts me, the wound from the traumatic event I had encountered is still fresh, but here I am, setting myself up for the worst as it might just happen again; no one who knows me would be able to track me down were this guy to do something with me, like kidnap, rape me or worse, traffic me or even butcher me. But still, I got into the car, as scared and as terrified as I was, I reassured myself; "not everyone I'll meet will turn out to be a perpetrator of rape or any kind of sexual assault or violence, let alone heartache towards me;

the world may be a dark and harsh place, but there still is a little good out there, some light shedders".

When we first met, I had a gut feeling that he was going to form some part of my life, although trusting your heart in a generation that has put a construed definition on the term of love as the "IT" factor, takes a lot of bravery, but I never thought that his place in my life would be the majority of my heart, I felt that I had no place left in me to love any longer, at least not a man. I want to be brutally honest, okay? And just say that for a minute there I had lost all hope for men, I could not put myself to believe that there were men out there who, although not entirely saints, still saw women as beautiful, strong, fierce & as a powerful force to be reckoned with, and wanted to, more than anything, protect them, love on them, and to build with them. I assumed that every guy I would meet would turn out to be the exact same douchebag as most of the men who had been present in my life before; deceiving, egotistical, manipulative, narcissistic liars, who are truly just imperfect human beings.

But I guess that wasn't the case at all. I was never stunned by the fact that a guy like him, abundant on his own, could be attracted to someone like me, bruised, still trying to heal from certain things I could never find the strength to discuss without shedding a tear or two, whether it be outwardly or internally, and that is because I still had that confidence in myself, I was and still am, fully "that woman",

One you could never resist, not because of her sex appeal or anything related to that,
but because of the aura she lets out,
there's something special about her, she is a force, and you ought to feel that.
You know there's a light inside of her that burns so bright, you can't help but be drawn closer to her, and it is nothing superstitious like that,
it's the very same light that was declared in the beginning of the ages, the same one the Creator leads his people with,
it has kept her heart warm through the aches, by torching through the cracks from her spirit,
it has kept her going, and for that reason; she has known that she is being led, led to something greater.

See, I have never known a love that looks beyond one's scars and flaws and is willing to take that leap of faith and build up something beautiful, at least not from the human heart. Because there I was, broken, trying to build myself up again, trying to figure out who I was, who I have been truly pieced to be, and with all that, beneath the brokenness, I found something worthwhile, I found me, and in finding myself, I was a magnet to that which felt aligned to my higher self, to what I was called for, and I know it sounds a little confusing to hear me say that "I found me" because isn't this supposed to be about me finding the missing piece to my puzzle, my soul mate? But won't you please just sit back, continue reading along, as you are soon to find out what is? Okay, thanks! Back to the story; perfect could never be the word I could use to describe him, because he was real, brutally real, and that is why I could not help but wonder, when I started getting to know him, "Could this be my forever? My happily ever after?".

Fortunately, no, I got burnt yet again *sighs*, I know I should just give up already, but hey now, it's things like love, we live and die for. Well, turns out he was a sweet talker who caressed my heart with sugar-coated lies. He was perfect, or at least the mask that he wore was, he made me believe every word that he had orchestrated from his mouth to sound like a musical note, it was a whole Do Re Mi Fa So La Ti Do show whenever he spoke to me, and I fell into a web, perfectly weaved with deceitful words. He thought he was a good guy even after he had caused me aches, tried to make me believe that he cared for me and that he never had ill-intentions for me. He still wanted to believe so much that he was a gentleman who didn't use, and abuse love out of selfishness, but here I was, a victim of his actions, he had lied to me. From the very first day we met, he was dishonest in his dealings with me, he made me believe that I was the one he wanted forever with, when in actual fact he was already invested elsewhere, and so through his deceit, he was a perpetrator of my pain, of yet again another heartache. And that was when it hit me, what exactly is a good person? Is he determined by his actions or good deeds, or is it just a state of being? In one of the previous chapters, I spoke about learning to separate an individual from their actions, which of course is not an easy thing to do because if you have good morals and values then why would you ever do something terrible, ever, to another human being? But the sad truth is that life is a bowl full of choices, difficult choices, which are sometimes influenced by external forces like temptation, greed, lust, etc. Take the wrong one, you're the bad guy. But see, we are all good people at one point, but it is our actions that are bad that lead to us being labelled the bad guy, a culprit of crime committed to another being. Therefore, we need to choose wisely, of course we are human and that means that we are not always going to do right by everyone, we will make mistakes because in this journey of self-discovery, lies a path of trial and error. But also, being human should never be used as an excuse to hurt other people because "you know as humans we make mistakes; we get tempted and we take the wrong decisions and, and, and...", no! Yeah sure, mistakes are going to be there, you are going to hurt people through your mistakes, but as a "human being", taking responsibility and accountability for your actions is also part of being human. At the end of the day, best believe that if you are truly genuine and honest in your dealings with other people, it is seldom that you will find yourself hurting other people, however if it does happen that you find yourself hurting someone; taking responsibility and humbling yourself, apologising and working towards being better by learning from those mistakes, deep down you remain a person who isn't so driven by their ego, but someone who realises that they are on a path of unlearning & relearning and is willing to take criticism as feedback, while actively working towards changing behaviours that are detrimental to the wellbeing of not only themselves, but of those around them, and that my friend, is what makes you good.

I just want to say that I love and hate pain all at the same time. Because although it forces you to really get out of your naive perception of how the world is, it also forces you to dig deeper into your soul and search it for that love that isn't subjected to any conditions. But it also ruins your relationships with those around you - trust issues. Being an individual who has been bruised & burnt a few times in both love & life, I find it difficult to distinguish between someone who is truly genuine in their intentions for me and someone who is just out to use & abuse me. Of course pain clouds our judgement sometimes, making us see the world through tainted eyes from our past hurts, betrayals & disappointments, but pain gives us this choice, it allows us to see the world as is, as this imperfect, messed up sphere filled with greedy people that need a whole lot of restoration, and yet gives us the choice of either becoming one with the world in its darkness, or being fuelled with the need to spread even more of our love & light into the world.

And so, does it really get any better? Well, I left that situation as well because I realised it wasn't meant for me, call me an escapist, will you? Maybe I'm the problem because "how do you keep encountering the same issues with different guys?" But I never will settle for anything less than what I deserve, hence, deciding to intentionally focus on my healing was my ultimate goal because I deserve to feel lighter and whole again. I saw it best to pour my own cup of magic into my own soul, because then and only then, would I be able to pour that same cup of magic out into the world – self love. This time around I chose me, I put myself first, and maybe that was the lesson, but to be honest? That felt truly amazing!

How I chose myself? It was on a random day, early in the morning when I was making my way to the bathroom for a morning shower of course, and that was when I bumped into someone, it was a familiar face, I swear I had seen them before, but I had just never paid them the attention. I was walking past a framed mirror when I saw them, I saw a reflection of them, and I remembered that this was where I had seen them before, I guess I was too busy or preoccupied with other things to even notice them, but this time around I had to stop, to stop and look. I saw them stare right back at me, that was when I fell in love, it was at first glance that I fell in love, I fell in love with the girl in the mirror, so strong yet so gentle, I saw her eyes penetrate my body right through to my soul, she knew me, she knew me because she was me, and so I fell in love with myself. For so long I had forgotten about this warrior who had been fighting day in and out to stay alive, who had been pushing boundaries to pursue her life's purpose even with the hurdles that had tripped her and had led her to breaking down, she never backed down, this was the girl whom life had thrown into the toilet pit and had decided that she was going to become the shit, she was the girl whom life threw to the ground but became one with the dirt, she was constantly adapting to the changes, she never gave up on me, she always stood by me, and this time around I had to choose her, I had to choose the girl who was choosing me over and over again, even when others wouldn't choose me. This time around, I chose me.

But of course, it wasn't just that one moment of realisation that made all the difference, choosing compassion towards myself was not easy, letting go wasn't easy either. I often reminisced over the good times we had, the good times we shared, but I had to remember the reason I had left in the first place, to remember the pain and sorrow those connections brought to me, I had to make a conscious decision daily to continuously choose me, even on my not so good days, even with the nasty feelings and emotions that often invaded my space, because the love of self isn't just a once off thing, it is progressive, it requires a whole lot of patience and brutal honesty with oneself, and so I had to ask myself a lot of questions during my self-care sessions;

1. How do you feel about this situation?
2. How did they make you feel?
3. What is it that you have learnt from your experiences?
4. What do you plan on doing better?

Some of the answers were that:

1. If I could look back to the rape for example; I feel that it was unfair, because why do I get to be the one who gets hurt, always? Yeah, I may have played a role in that by being a little too naïve and trusting, but is it truly a bad thing for wanting to see the world in a better light? Either way, I know it wasn't my fault, my perpetrator had his own sicko motives, those were what led to him initiating the act, and even if I weren't too naïve or too trusting, that would not change the fact that he thought of doing it to begin with, he just has deeper issues that lie within.

2. With regards to the connections I have made with past lovers who betrayed my love, I feel used and disappointed,

perhaps I was a bit too idealistic in my expectations of love with them, but that is not an excuse for how they treated me, it isn't my fault that they are disloyal men who cheat, lie and use love to their own advantage, yes, I can be too giving sometimes, well, all the time, and that is perhaps because I give what I long to receive, the love, the affection, I over-give and over-love not only because I know how it feels to lack, but because I have so much to offer, I always see the best in others and hope that they too can, but not everyone deserves that.

3. All these encounters and connections I have had may have bruised me a lot, but I have learnt so much from these, when it comes to closure; I have learnt that sometimes you are never going to receive the answers that you seek, and as humans, our first instinct is to always assume the worst out of the people who have hurt us because hating is so easy. But to love? To love means that you are willing to forgive some of these individuals even without receiving any kind of apology, remorse, or even an explanation from them, and that is difficult, to just be like "oh well, shit happens but life goes on", and not feel like you want to choke the life out of them whenever you come across them, or even just hear their name or are just reminded of them, that takes grace, and not many are brave enough to show courtesy to those who have hurt them. Remember; moving on and letting go are two different things, someone can say they are moving on from someone or something, mainly because they do not have a choice but

to do that; to exit someone's life maybe because this person is not willing to change, and a lot of us do that, we break up with partners and move on to new connections, but have we let go? Letting go is when you release the weight you have carried from that connection, the anger this individual may have caused you, the disappointment, the mental exhaustions.

4. To be honest, I believe that I too may have had some abandonment issues and negative attachment styles; I feared giving so much of myself to someone and have them take it for granted, even worse, take me for granted. I did not want to lose something that I had grown fond of, my little ego would get bruised, hence my actions of over giving and over loving in hopes that the person on the receiving end would recognise my sincerity, generosity, and efforts, and decide to stay because "she is a good person". But through the connections I have made, I have had to take a few Ls – Lessons; I have had to learn to not stretch myself so much for someone, just to show that I love them, that romantic love is a two-way street and although love should be unconditional, I deserve a partner who matches my energy, who will be on the same wavelength as me – reciprocity. I have also learnt that within a relationship; I need to maintain my own independence, yes, I see romantic love as an act of merging two souls into one, but I have made peace with the fact that my partner and I are two separate entities, and as much as love brings us closer, it is a partnership,

and a partnership involves two people coming into an agreement to build and to work on something solid. Once I began to understand these things, I became less attached to the idea of dependence on my partner to feel loved, I stopped trying so hard to control the outcome in any of my connections, and just started believing that if something truly is meant to be then it will work out in the end. I was able to accept the ending of any connection with partners, without holding on so much to the idea of what could've been or should've been. I stopped chasing and started attracting. I let go of pain and anger from my trauma, when I started to understand that sometimes we are torches that light up the inner struggles and wounds of other individuals, and vice versa.

That is what I have chosen for myself and will continue to choose for myself.

I used to be an insecure little girl, who did not fully understand her worth, let alone the concept of what it means to love and to be loved in a romantic sense, but life happened, not only once and most definitely not twice, and I guess that was my learning field. Life humbled me in the most painful of ways, but one of the most beautiful things that came out that pain were the lessons that life taught me. I learnt the hard way, but boy did I learn a lot. I began to look at situations, things, and people around me with not only just one set of eyes, but I looked at situations and people from different angles and views; the rear view, the front view, back view, and side view and could then draw conclusions and make a decision. I realized so much that made me stop taking things personal, not just in romantic relationships but life in general.

Life changed my perspective and my views but I'm glad it did not take away myself from me.

Thus, moving forward, I will trust my intuition more, I will set more healthy boundaries and stick to them. I will learn to leave situations that do not serve me but only steal from me, not later but as soon as I realize it. I will love myself a little more and put myself first.

It was and still is a lot of hard-core labour, but I am happy with the progress I have made thus far, and that is why I can say "It does get better".

CHAPTER 17- MESSAGES TO HER

Letter to the inner child

Dear young one,

I know life hasn't been easy on you,
Born into a vicious world, your soul was just so pure & innocent.
The world was too fast paced for your kind.

xxx P.S. Never let your experiences change who you have always been; soulful, playful, and vibrant *xxx*

Sweet, Sweet Medicine

Remain that sweet medicine,
Healing souls that have been shattered.
The world hasn't been fair to you,
You have had to deal with things that no kind soul ever has to,
But regardless, you should never stop dripping your sweet Golden
Bee Syrup onto the deep core of this world.
After all, you are that sweet medicine.

<u>Nursing a wounded soul</u>

With this honey, I submerge every wound and every ache,

To transform and to renew, this soul which was once beautiful but has now become shattered by false promises from another Man's tongue.

With this warmth of affection, I extend a love from self, to penetrate deep into the roots of this dried up soul's stream from the tears shed because of bruises caused by a Man's action of betrayal & disappointment, in turn stunting its growth.

With the power vested deep inside of me I say; Heal soul, sweet soul, permeate your cracks with that bit of light left inside of you, you are Golden after all.

To the Feminal Being who believes that ALL men are trash

This is a reminder for her; you may not have had a great start when
it came to any relationship
department with a man, but I want you to
remember this;
Not all men are trash! You will someday meet a
masculine Being who will love, respect and be
gentle with your soul. He will not try to be
dominant over you, but will recognise that you
are equals. He will treat you like the Princess that you
are, because Your Royal Highness, that's who
you are! He will recognise your flaws and accept
you as you are because he is also not perfect.
So, until then, do not stop loving and respecting
men, all in the name of "Men are Trash".

To the men who were too shallow for her kind;

But Creatures like her are meant to be SBWLed(craved) from a distance,
Because once you get too close to her,
You realise that she is intense.
Intense in the way she feels, and intense in the way she loves.
She is intense in her emotions, and in the thoughts contained in her brain.

And so, if you aren't drawn to such intensity, she may come off as alien to you.

To the Individual who thinks turning off the switch/unplugging the plug is the best answer for all of this, because "you don't and won't have to deal with any of it";

"Lights off" is not the answer, my darling!
I know you are tired but
You are stronger than you give yourself credit.
You can go through this and come out even stronger or
wiser. Just don't do it, don't pull the plug as yet.
It is not yet your time of departure.
You are a story yet to be told!

Don't you fucking quit

On yourself.
I know you hear it all the time,
'Hang on, hang in there, it will be all right, just keep hanging tight.' *Smiley face and heart*
But what do you do when you are hanging onto dear life's last thread?
What do you do when you have got no fight left inside of you?
What do you do when it feels as though you keep hitting walls in every turn you take?
What do you do when it feels like you have just taken your last breath?
When it feels as though there is nothing left worth living for?
Well, you keep gasping for that air,
You keep fighting,
You keep hanging, you don't let go,
I know you're strong because I'm strong too,
I know you are worth the chance, and that you're worth fighting for, you are a big deal, you may just not know it yet.
So, don't you ever quit on yourself.

Hiding Place

But you could never hide away your light,

Because just like in Matthew 5:14;

You are the light of the world that cannot be hidden.

Light Bearer

But you cannot hide away your truths,
You are the light bearer,
Here to illuminate the darkness,
And to shed some of your light onto the dark souls of
this earth.
So, keep shining, even in the darkest night.

Wet pillows

I've seen your cries,
From the dampened case of your pillow, I know
You have buried your face deep within your pillow,
Afraid to attract attention by crying out too loud,
I have watched you in the silence of your cries,
soothing yourself to sleep, with a blocked nose
that made you sound like you had almost caught a fever,
But do not fret, these wet pillows are symbol of
your strength, every tear drop that has hit its
fabric has been a sign of your healing.
The floods will soon subside, and when they do, you will flower.

A story yet to be told

You are not just a fraction in a statistic of the number of victims of Assault,
Your story is one of a kind,
One of a survivor who never backed down because they were stripped off their dignity,
But became a rescue to those who could not sway through the experience.
Your story deserves to be shared.

Take your power back

"They" i.e., your perpetrator, pain and trauma may have had a grip
on your body and mind for a little while;
But never allow them to steal your soul's strength,
The soul is where your power rests,
So, take your power back!

Closure is

"Regardless of the outcome,
My life will continue.
I will not remain stagnant or stuck, just because I haven't received any answers on why it happened or an apology for why they did it.
The only closure I am going to receive is the peace I allow into myself by letting go of the anger.
They will not give me closure."

Accountability & Responsibility

Holding others accountable for their actions, and taking responsibility for your own actions sets both you and the other person free,
Free from the victim mentality you might want to carry around so that people feel sorry for you, and
Free from any toxic behaviour, trait or weakness stemming from either one of your guys' being,
Do not be afraid to speak out.

It is not your fault

Remember;
Rape or Abuse is not as a result of what you initiated,
It is forced action that comes with a lack of consent.
It is a weakness on your perpetrators part to hold themselves back
when urged, an inner struggle for them,
It never is your fault.

Communication

Communication to persons whose actions may have caused you
or brought you any form of ache, is necessary.
Not only for your wellbeing,
But to make the other individual aware of their weaknesses and
faults, and how to work towards bettering themselves,
You can't force them to change, but you can only point them in
the direction of change, through communicating.

P.S. Your summer is near

To my Baby,
In the past couple of breaths,
You may have had so many winters than expected,
Not to mention the unplanned encounters that left you shaking!
You got bruised along the way,
You have been disappointed quite a lot,
You have been forced to be strong and to step out of your natural habitat,
And as much as it has been feeling dreadful to be in this season,
You have made countless connections, none of which you should regret,
Because through them;
You've been learning, healing, and most importantly growing!

Please.

Please Heal.
Please let go of the denial that you are not hurting.
Please do some internal work within to get your soul back,
Not back to its original state, but to a place
where you can function well in this new.
Please do it for you.

<u>Laughter & Time do heal wounds.</u>

And by now you thought you'd be okay,
You thought you would have had the whole experience out of
your system,
That thinking about it wouldn't hurt as much as it did before,
But that's not how it be,
It takes a while; healing takes time, but you have to do the work.

The struggle to healing

You begin to realise that healing is a life-long process,
You realise that your bruises and scars still need more time to be
nursed,
But daily you try, you try to move on, you try to forget,
But your weary torn apart heart bleeds a little more when it's
triggered.
The thought of it all brings you sick to your stomach,
But you realise that it's okay to feel this way, that "it be like that
sometimes".

You do heal

The healing process may take some time,
You can never explain when exactly you get healed,
But during the process, it may feel a little hard, a little wrecking,
and a little disheartening,
But eventually you get there,
You do heal.

You are Healer

You have the ability to channel your pain into
some form of art, to allow your tears to cleanse
the scars from your pain, and water the streams
of your soul that were once dried up as a result
of the hurt. You have the ability to heal yourself.
You are of a Healer, and that just means that you too are a healer.
Healing is not external of you, it's within you,
You need to dig deeper within yourself to find healing.

Healing Aura

Guard your heart,
Replenish your soul,
You cannot live on an empty stomach, just like you can't bloom
on dry land.
Feed your mind with that which is flourishing,
Allow your cup to runneth over,
But don't be surprised if you attract broken souls,
You are a beacon of light, a pathway to a brighter place, protect
your aura.

How do you guard your heart?

How do you guard your heart when all you really want to do is love? To love from the deepest core of your Being,

How do you shield your heart? From the pain and disappointment caused by another human's actions,

How do you keep it safe? Well, I don't know because all I want is to give a love that is whole and not just a piece of it, I just want to experience the total bliss of being loved and cared for by someone else, and returning the same gesture, but how?

How do I only give just a piece of me? Because see, I am whole, and being whole means that I am not lacking, being whole means that I give from my entirety. So, how on earth am I expected to ever give love while holding some of it back?

Construed View made new

I pray rain drops of truth cleanse your eyes and
remove your view of the world through tainted
eyes, just so you can learn to feel the light
brightening up your soul, reminding you to shed
some of your very own light onto the world, as it's
needed.

<u>Freedom</u>

fri^dom

(noun)

A feeling of annihilating anything that hinders one
from truly & fully expressing one's highest Self.
As you let go of your pain & hurt,
you start to experience the freedom of living life
as your highest Self.

Plot Twist

The best stories always have a plot twist,
Something unexpected that leaves the audience astonished and in
awe of the fact that the writer would play with their minds like
that,
Something along the lines of "we thought we knew exactly how
this story was going and how it would end, but never expected
'that' or 'this' to happen, well at least not in 'that' way, and now
we realise that it was necessary and it made the story even more
interesting and exciting, and although confusing at some point, it
has been like a little adventure we were put on, and it was so darn
worth it."

Lost Souls

But aren't we all a little broken?

Seeking some light to come warm up our hearts from the coldness it has resorted to? Are we not tired of not knowing whether we are on the right path?

Praying for a sign from the heavens as reassurance to keep going? Perhaps we all just want a little reminder here and there, now and again, of who we truly are? Maybe we are sometimes confused because truth is, we're all a little lost in this chaos called life, born into a world that teaches us rules that we eventually have to unlearn. We are all born only to try and find our way back to ourselves.

So, do yourself a favour and find your own way back home.

Freewill

Maybe after all, life is about choosing;
Choosing who we are despite the many standards that have been set for us to sort of direct the way we should act, and interact with others;
To choose who we'd like to be and sticking with that even through the redefinitions.
Choosing who we want and sticking with them;
Perhaps at the end of the day, the choice is ours to make and it shouldn't be based off of the opinions of others that try to define and constrain us;
Maybe life truly is what you make of it, but even so, whatever you choose, let it be good.

Blindfolds off

With all the pain and ache that's been coming at you,
The only thing you can use to fight with, is love,
a Love into self,
After all, the world was never perfect, and
I guess this was you learning to see the world for what it truly is.

The girl before the pain:

I met a girl once; she was kind, sweet and gentle.
She never said much, all she ever did was laugh, smile, and exude happiness, she had a sense of freedom to her.
But it wasn't long enough after those few encounters I had with her, that she was never to be found.
She was left unrecognisable, her soul was bruised, her innocence?
- Stolen.
All because of the greed of selfish lovers and Men.

I miss that girl, but I know that although I could never get the same girl back, I have found a matured version of her.

Through the pain and not because of it, she has become strong, and although she may have tripped and fallen for a while, she was able to pick herself up again, to brush off the dirt and keep it moving. And so, I realise that I had never lost her to begin with, I was always looking up, forgetting that we all do touch the ground every once in a while, but it is our ability to pick ourselves up again that makes us strong.

P.S. My name is Murendeni Matumba, best referred to as "Ms Rendy", and I hope to shed some light on the root cause of some of the gruesome behaviour towards our daughters & sons by the men we have entrusted our care to, by choosing not only justice but choosing to change the narrative on woman and child abuse, on gender-based violence. With every problem, there is always a root cause that needs to be dealt with, and until we find and deal with it, the number of cases of sexual assault and any form of violence against our daughters by men, will not cease to increase!

NB: These are my thoughts and opinions, based off experience and observations, not a personal attack on Men, let alone anyone.

www.ingramcontent.com/pod-product-compliance
Lightning Source LLC
Chambersburg PA
CBHW022020240626
47154CB00007B/2186